87997-UE1982 • (CANADA $2.95) • U.S. $2.50

DA
DAW
FANTASY
No. 607

LIN C

DRAGO

AN ADULT FANTASY

D0030711

THE CAST OF CHARACTERS

ARIMASPIA: *Princess of Scythia and our heroine.*

ATLANTES: *the famous Wizard of the Pyrenees.*

CALLIPYGIA: *daughter of the Queen of the Amazons.*

CONCALINE: *a wicked Fairy.*

FELIXMARTE: *a lovesick young knight of Hyrcania.*

GAGLIOFFO: *a repentent Paynim, formerly a scoundrel.*

GRUMEDAN: *an evil enchanter.*

KESRICK: *a Frankish knight, and our hero.*

LUNETTA: *a Princess under an enchantment.*

MANDRICARDO: *a stalwart knight of Tartary.*

PIROUETTA: *Sir Kesrick's fairy godmother.*

ST. COLMAN: *an Irish saint who likes messing about in boats.*

THUNDERTHIGHS: *a Giant with an appetite for Meat.*

Plus:

Fastiticalon the giant Sea-Tortoise; Brigadore the Hippogriff; a couple of Wyverns; Another Giant; the Monoceros; and a grateful Dragon.

THE SCENE: Terra Magica, a parallel world whose geography and history has become the source of our myths, epics and fairy tales.

THE TIME is the Twilight of the Golden Age.

LIN CARTER
DRAGONROUGE

Further Adventures in Terra Magica

DAW BOOKS, INC.

DONALD A. WOLLHEIM, PUBLISHER

1633 Broadway, New York, NY 10019

Copyright ©, 1984, by Lin Carter.
All Rights Reserved.
Cover art and frontispiece by Ken W. Kelly.

DEDICATION

*To the memory of two of my
favorite of all fantasy writers:
T.H. White and Andrew Lang.*

First Printing, December 1984

1 2 3 4 5 6 7 8 9

PRINTED IN U.S.A.

CONTENTS

BOOK ONE

BOOK ONE

———

PIRATES AND MONSTERS

1

The Burning Sands

It was the noontide and the sun stood at the zenith, pouring down scorching rays from a cloudless sky like an immense copper bowl heated in a furnace. Below, dry gullies split the desert sands of the Moghrab with zigzag cracks. The desert was littered with the skulls and bones of men and acrawl with hairy black spiders, scarlet scorpions and deadly yellow vipers.

In these barren parts of the Kingdom of Mauretania few men cared to live, hence it would have surprised the onlooker—had there been anyone else about—to observe in the distance two four-footed steeds, each bearing two riders. As the travelers came nearer, they would have surprised our hypothetical viewer even more, for they were a curious party.

In the fore rode a young Frankish knight with dark red hair and mischievous green eyes sparkling in his tanned and handsome face. A

9

long sword slept in its scabbard at his thigh,
and the knightly emblem of a red dragon was
blazoned upon his surcoat and his shield, which
dangled from a peg on the saddle. This was the
famous Sir Kesrick of Dragonrouge, the hero of
many knightly adventures, who had most recently served the wicked Egyptian wizard, Zazamanc, the just desserts of his innumerable
villainies.

Before Kesrick in the capacious saddle rode
a beautiful, and quite unclothed, young woman
with long golden hair and wide, violet eyes
like amethysts of the purest hue. She was none
other than the Scythian Princess, Arimaspia,
whom Sir Kesrick had earlier rescued from a
ferocious sea-monster called the Rosmarin.

And the steed upon which the pair rode was
a Hippogriff from the famous stables of the
sorcerer Atlantes. This remarkable creature
had the body and legs of a horse, but the
beaked head, broad wings and clawed feet of
an eagle.

His name was Brigadore.

A little ways behind these two, another pair
rode mounted upon a gigantic black warhorse
whose name was Bayardetto. The man who
held the reins was swarthy and mustached and
clad in knightly armor; he was a Tartar knight
named Mandricardo, the son of King Agricane
of that nation, and instead of a surcoat his
flashing mail was covered with the skins of
lions he had slain in the wildernesses of Tartary.

Before him, and cradled in his arms with her
head nestled comfortably against his shoulder,

The Burning Sands

rode a young woman. She was dressed in bits of armor—gilded bronze greaves and buskins and a sort of abbreviated kilt of leather straps studded with pieces of metal—but mostly she was bare and a damsel of ample, if not heroic, proportions. Her name was Callipygia, and she was one of the seventeen daughters of the Queen of Amazonia in the farther parts of Asia.

As for how these four people all got together and faced many perils and became fast friends, I will say nothing here, but if you wish to learn more about them and their histories, I recommend to your attention a book of mine called Kesrick*, in which their stories are told.

Only a little while before they had left the underground palace of the Egyptian magician—which had once been the residence of another wicked sorcerer called the Moghrabi Sufrah, who for a time pretended to be the uncle of the present Emperor Aladdin of China—and were riding north for the sea. Mandricardo and the Amazon girl had decided to help Sir Kesrick and the Princess of Scythia return to Kesrick's ancestral home, Dragonrouge, in the land of the Franks.

They were not able to decide exactly how to get there. Mandricardo thought they should ride east into Numidia and ask the loan of a ship from King Fayoles. Kesrick did not wish to travel so far out of his way.

"It would take us days to ride to the capital of Numidia," he argued, "when we can just as

*Kesrick, by Lin Carter; DAW Books, New York, 1982.

easily find a ship in one of the seaports along the coast of Mauretania. True, I know nothing about the present king of that country, but we don't need to ask him for favors, anyway." And here he slapped, with a significant gesture, the bulging saddlebags slung across the withers of the Hippogriff. They were stuffed with rubies.

"It would be nice if the Wandering Garden of Wotzername—" began Callipygia.

"—Acrasia," said Arimaspia.

"—Acrasia," repeated the Amazon. "Would turn up again," she continued. "Then we could travel to Frankland in comfort." She sighed, remembering the limpid water of the pool amidst the trees of the enchanted flying garden, otherwise known as "the Bower of Bliss." She would certainly enjoy a cool bath after all this sand and scorching sunlight.

Mandricardo disagreed. "Not so, beloved, by my troth!" he declared stoutly. "And miss all the adventures along the way? Why, dash it all, Cally, there may be any number of princesses under enchantment or damsels in durance vile or evil enchanters we may yet encounter! Stirs the soul of chivalry in a knight errant, eh, Kesrick, old man?"

"I suppose so," said Kesrick noncommittally. Privately, he thought to himself that if it had only been he and Arimaspia, the Hippogriff could quite easily have flown them home to Dragonrouge. But he was too tactful to say this aloud, and had no wish to hurt his friend's feelings.

They rode along for a time, while snakes and

The Burning Sands

spiders and scorpions slithered or crawled or scuttled hastily from underfoot, and the noontide sun continued to blaze down, as if desirous of broiling the surface of Terra Magica into cinders.

"I can't help wondering whatever happened to Gaglioffo," mused Arimaspia after a time. Mandricardo ground his teeth and growled the names of two or three of the less respectable of the gods worshipped in Tartary.

"*That* treacherous Paynim!" he exclaimed savagely. "By my halidom, but who cares, what?"

"By Pappaeus, I know!" said Arimaspia. "But all the same. He wasn't anywhere around when we were leaving the underground palace of Zazamanc, or if he was, he was hiding. . . ."

The rascally Gaglioffo, whom they had earlier rescued from an enchantment, had frequently been (as Sir Mandricardo liked to put it) "a thorn in their foot and a stitch in their side, what?" during several of their adventures.

"Just what *is* a halidom, anyway, do you happen to know?" asked Kesrick, changing the subject. The Tartar shrugged.

"Dashed if *I* know, old chap! Just something by which we knights errant often swear," he said carelessly.

They rode on across the burning desert, still arguing whether they should turn east toward Numidia or continue straight ahead for Mauretania, in order to cross the Middle Sea by ship.

Gaglioffo, in the meanwhile, was having a terrible time. The ugly little Paynim, with goggling

13

eyes and bandy-legs and blubbery lips, had indeed hidden out of sight during the departure of our heroes. He guiltily assumed that the fearless knights would have dispatched him with their shining swords, in recompense for his many villainies and betrayals of their trust and kindness. Now he found himself alone in the deserted subterranean castle of the Egyptian wizard, who had been transformed by one of his own backfiring magic spells into a remarkably unattractive marble statue.

After quite a time, which he devoted to whimpering and snuffling and to feeling sorry for himself in general, the dwarfish Paynim tried to think of what he should do next. Not having a steed, he could hardly hope to survive the long journey on foot across the blistering sands of the Mohgrab. But, then, neither could he stay here in these dank and dripping caverns, alone and slowly starving.

You see, a careless housekeeper like most bachelors, Zazamanc never bothered to make even a pretense of stocking the larder or replenishing the pantry. Instead, when he wanted a meal, the magician had conjured one out of empty air—an art which the unfortunate Gaglioffo did not possess, but one which would have certainly come in handy.

Only one mode of escape presented itself to Gaglioffo's wits (such as they were), and it was a form of transport which made him quake to the depths of his cowardly heart. That is, there still remained in the underground caverns the flying iron chariot which Zazamanc had used

The Burning Sands

to range up and down the world in the perpetrating of his villainies.

This unusual conveyance was drawn through the skies by a matched team of winged and dragonish Wyverns. During his trips in the aerial chariot, Gaglioffo had watched the magician carefully, despite his terror, and had memorized how to operate the chariot. Now, after Zazamanc had been transmogrified into a marble statue, the Princess Arimaspia had kindheartedly freed all of the denizens in the magician's menagerie of monsters, including the twin Wyverns. However, the Wyverns had come flapping home by now on their tireless batlike wings, more accustomed to the underground palace than to any other abode, and, at this very moment, were hungrily devouring some wriggling serpents and other vermin on the sands before the entrance to the cavern. They chewed down their repulsive luncheon noisily and with every sign of finding the meal delicious.

Gaglioffo screwed up what little courage he possessed, which was not very much, and, calling upon his idols, Mahoum and Golfarin, the Nephew of Mahoum, not to mention the redoubtable Termagant, he subdued the hissing Wyverns by stammering the words Zazamanc had used, and harnessed the creatures to the chariot.

Erelong, the Wyverns bore the chariot aloft at a sickeningly steep angle, with the Paynim cowering and blubbering with fear, and rather happy that he *had* found nothing to eat in the underground palace. For, if he had eaten, the flight was so rapid and precipitous that he would certainly have lost his lunch.

Whistling through the air, the iron chariot bore Gaglioffo through the skies and across the burning sands.

2

The Bucket o' Blood

By nightfall, the four travelers had reached the shores of the Middle Sea and found themselves, not in Mauretania as they had anticipated, for that country was a little farther west, but in one of the seacoast towns of another country called Mezzoramia, concerning which they knew nothing.

The town, however, was quaint and cozy, with cobbled streets and snug cottages, and long wharves that thrust out into the blue water and afforded a safe anchorage of many ships.

"Oh, by Jove! The bounding main, what? How jolly!" exclaimed Sir Mandricardo, expanding his chest and drinking in the salt sea breeze zestfully. He knew nothing whatsoever about sailing, but declined to mention the fact.

Kesrick had spied an inn with adjoining stables, so they guided their steeds in that direction and dismounted. A scrawny stableboy with a runny nose gasped at the unearthly Hippogriff and gaped, drooling, at the naked beauty of the Scythian Princess, but accepted a flung coin and promised to groom, water and feed Kesrick's steed and Bayardetto.

As they entered the hostelry, Mandricardo read the name above the door. "Good-oh! 'The Bucket o' Blood,' jolly old nautical term, I'll warrant!" he cried happily. Again, Kesrick said nothing, but he exchanged a meaningful glance with Arimaspia: to him, as to her, the inn's name sounded like the disreputable hangout of pirates, corsairs, buccaneers, and other sea-going robbers.

However, they had already paid the stable-boy to care for their steeds, and it was too late now to change inns. So they strode in, finding a long, low-roofed room crowded with benches and trestle-tables. Here were sprawled or seated a ruffianly looking number of old salts, thumping their mugs of grog in time to a rude sea chantey which some of them bawled at the top of their lungs.

"Don't know the words, meself," Mandricardo advised Callipygia in low tones. "Just hum along."

But the song died on every lip as the oddly dressed foursome entered the Bucket o' Blood. Furtive eyes studied them narrowly; hoarse whispers were exchanged behind callused hands. It would seem that Mezzoramia seldom gave its hospitality to Frankish or Tartar knights, or Amazonian or Scythian princesses.

Most of the seamen had scarlet kerchiefs wound about their brows; gold hoops bobbled from pierced lobes; many wore a hook instead

The Bucket o' Blood

of a hand, or a pegleg where a leg of bone and flesh should properly be. They had stubbled cheeks or bristling beards and were attired in the stained red coats of admirals. Dirks and dags bristled: some of these were thrust into sashes or cummerbunds or broad leathern belts, others were stuck in the top of seaboots.

Pistols had not been invented yet.*

Arimaspia looked around. Strings of onions and red peppers dangled from hooks in the tarry rafters; a huge fire roared on the stone grate across the room, where a whole bullock slowly turned on the spit, which was being worked by the veritable twin of the scrawny stableboy, identical even to the runny nose. The delicious odor of cooking food permeated the smoky air.

The barkeep, who seemed also to be the cook, came stumping out to greet them. His left leg was cut off at the hip and he leaned on a wooden crutch. He was a stocky fellow with stubbled cheeks, and a face as broad and red as a ham, with a gorgeous parrot riding on one husky shoulder. Wiping greasy hands on an even greasier apron, he knuckled his brow obsequiously, bowing and scraping.

"Sit 'e doon, squires 'n' ladies, a table t' starboard, if 'e please! Arr. A drap o' wine ter begin wiv? Arr. Look alive, lad—fetch a bottle o' me best wine fer th' gentry over yere," said this individual

They seated themselves at a long table which

---

*But gunpowder was even then beginning to be experimented with in the regions of the Grand Cham.

had been crowded by mariners, who were politely asked to move in the simplest and most practical manner: that is, Mine Host of the Bucket o' Blood upended the benches, spilling the riffraff onto the floor. They grumbled a bit and showed their teeth nastily, but, oddly enough, did not make further or more physical objection to this rudeness.

Before long, the travelers were munching down smoking beef, garnished with potatoes, onions, carrots and peppers, the whole a-swim in delicious spiced gravy, with the sort of appetite that comes only from a day in the saddle, toiling across the burning wastes.

The wine was decent enough, too.

They spent that night at the inn, hiring rooms on the second floor. The accommodations offered by the Bucket o' Blood were bare cubicles and not much more: low-ceilinged (so low that the two knights had to stoop over to walk about), equipped only with cots whose mattresses were stuffed with straw, a rickety table, a wobble-footed chair, a stump of candle in a cracked dish, and a chamberpot in the corner. Still, the four discovered how easy it is to sleep even under such primitive conditions, after a day in the saddle and a good, solid meal, well furnished with a few bottles of decent wine.

Kesrick discovered that Sir Mandricardo snored.

Next morning, after a rasher of bacon and a dozen scrambled eggs, the four were up and out to procure passage for themselves and their steeds on one or another of the ships in the

The Bucket o' Blood

harbor. It was a bright, breezy day: gulls uttered raucous cries like doors on rusty hinges, swooping and hovering in the gusty air; the harbor smelled, not unpleasantly, of rotting fishheads, tar, creosote, sun-baked canvas, dried salt, seasoned wood.

Ships from many ports were in harbor that morning; the four friends vied with each other to see who could identify the most different vessels. Arimaspia correctly pointed out a strange ship from the dominions of the Grand Cham by its bat-ribbed sails of waxed parchment. The Tartar knight spotted a ship from distant Thule, which he recognized by its sleek black hull and sails of rich tapestry. Sir Kesrick had no difficulty in pointing out a slim galleon from the half-sunken city of Ys, and a gigantic quinquadrime from Tarshish, while Callipygia alone was able to pick out a swag-bellied cargo vessel from Mogadore, loaded to the gunnels with teakwood, copra, tea, and smaragdines. The contest, then, resulted in a draw—or would have, until Arimaspia identified a dragon-prowed ship with red and yellow striped sails, which hailed from either Valhalla or Jotunheim.

She thought Jotunheim, for the half-naked seamen were immense, taller even than Mandricardo, with pale white skins and bushy beards and manes of blond hair so pale as to be flaxen. Everyone knows, the Aesir had red or dark gold hair.

By noon they had procured passages for themselves and their steeds on a lean, rakish vessel with the ominous-sounding name of "the Jolly

Roger." Its captain, a jovial but weasel-eyed, scoundrely mariner, rejoiced in the name of Flint. It had been Mine Host of the Bucket o' Blood who brought him and his ship to their attention. When they returned to the inn for the noonday meal, they found the two huddled at the rear of the main room in whispered conversation. Kesrick did not feel easy with Flint, having heard Mine Host mumble something about "gert leather bags what clink 'n' clank," but resolved to go along with Flint's offer.

After all, they had just wasted the morning being turned down by skipper after skipper, for no one they had talked to was willing to transport a warhorse. Much less, a Hippogriff.

Flint did not seem to mind at all. In fact, he seemed eager to be of service to them.

"Have to keep our eyes on that fellow," Kesrick muttered to Mandricardo. "I don't at *all* care for his looks ... and, if anything, his crew are an even more rascally troop of verminous scallawags."

"Scum of the Seven Seas." Mandricardo nodded soberly.

"What exactly *are* the Seven Seas, Mandro?" inquired the Amazon girl interestedly. "I can only think of about three, maybe four."

"Well, ah," began the Tartar. "Let me see, now; 'pon my soul! There's, um, Whatzisname ... and the one down south of everything, and ... and ..."

They were set to depart shortly before sundown, as Flint desired to catch the evening tide. So

The Bucket o' Blood

they settled their accounts with their host, who seemed more than delighted to accept a pigeons-blood ruby the size of the skull of a domestic cat, in lieu of the local coinage. They tossed their last copper to the stableboy, who had certainly done a fine job of grooming Bayardetto, whose sleek black hide glistened like waxed ebony, and Brigadore, whose bronze plumage shone as never before.

They got the two beasts aboard, although Brigadore did not like the gangplank and Bayardetto mightily distrusted the bamboo cage into which the sailors alternately tugged and pushed him. Then they bore their own luggage and saddlebags into the stateroom Flint had assigned to them, not, of course, forgetting the twin sacks of rubies.

Then—carefully locking the cabin door—they went on deck to watch the sailors make preparations for embarking. Kesrick found them as dastardly looking a lot as he had expected, but the practiced ease with which they swarmed in the shrouds and untacked the canvas impressed him that, ugly group or not, they knew their business when it came to seamanship. He made some remark on this to Mandricardo, who glumly answered, "Um."

Kesrick glanced at his companion. The Tartar was clutching the rail with such intensity that his knuckles showed bone-white even through his swarthy skin. His face, however, looked a trifle greenish.

"Is all well with you?" inquired the Frankish knight solicitously.

Mandricardo nodded vigorously, attempted a

hearty grin, bent over the rail and noisily lost his dinner overboard. As Kesrick assisted his friend below, the mariners in the rigging chuckled. It was probably the first time any of them had seen a passenger get seasick before the ship had even left its harbor.

"Sickly bunch o' landlubbers, I say," cackled one wizened old sea rogue to his comrade. The other leered knowingly, revealing teeth filed to points.

"Wealthy bunch, I say, matey," he hissed. "Did 'e lay yer lamps on them two gert sacks? Stuffed t' th' scuppers wiv rubies, they say. Rubies bigger'n mangoes . . ."

"Up anchor, ye swabs, an' look alive, now!" Flint bellowed from the afterdeck in a lusty voice.

The *Jolly Roger* turned her prow into the north; wind bellied in her ochre sails as she set slowly out into the chilly waters of the Middle Sea of the world.

3

The Mysterious Island

Toward midnight, or a little before, their ship
ran into a thick bank of fog. It was so thick, the
clammy, swirling stuff, that about all you *could*
see was your hand in front of your face, contrary to the familiar saying.

Mandricardo, who had by then already lost
his supper, his lunch, and his breakfast, climbed
up the gangway to the deck to see if he could
get rid of any of yesterday's meals, as well. He
returned to report that the *Jolly Roger* had
slowed to a crawl.

"Why, I wonder?" mused Sir Kesrick. "Flint
can hardly be afraid of running into another
ship, in the midst of all these waters. The chance
of one vessel running into another in open sea
must be highly unlikely."

"There are always *sea-monsters*, of course,"
said Mandricardo pessimistically. The Tartar
knight had by now formed a definite dislike of

maritime travel. It was horseback or nothing for him, from this point on.

Just then the *Jolly Roger* ran into something with a shudder that made every timber in her hull groan in protest. Crockery fell in the galley; men tumbled like tenpins all over the decks and rose with alarmed and barbarous oaths on their lips. The foresail came crashing down like thunder. Bayardetto neighed piercingly and began kicking out the bars of his bamboo cage.

Kesrick got dressed and hurried on deck. The fog was a dim blanket of grayness that closed about him like an immense but palpable fist, cutting off nearly every sense. Men were running about, shouting to each other, bare heels thudding on the deck, which, the Frankish knight noticed uncomfortably, was *tilted* at an unusual degree.

He looked about to find someone in a position of authority from whom he could demand an explanation, but could recognize no one in the milling crowd. Then, leaning over the rail and straining his eyes, he saw something dead ahead. It was a shallow, dark curve of something—a low island perhaps.

The ship had run aground!

But—how could that be? Flint had plotted a course due north from Mezzoramia to the seacoast of Bohemia on the mainland. And Sir Kesrick had studied the chart: there were no islands in the way.

A sickening gurgle came from below-decks. The deck listed even more.

"Shiver me timbers, but the ol' gel's takin' water," roared a familiar foghorn voice, Flint's.

The Mysterious Island

"Into th' boats, me hearties! It's ivvery man fer himse'f!"

They were all dressed by now, save, of course, Arimaspia, and had brought all of their luggage on deck. The Scythian Princess looked around, rather appalled.

"Oh, Detosyrus, are we sinking?" she wailed, clutching Sir Kesrick's arm.

"Looks like it," remarked that worthy, gloomily.

Sir Mandricardo wistfully contemplated the long years of his life which had been happily spent ashore; dry land never appealed to him more than at this moment. There, the only hazards or discomforts to be encountered by a wandering knight-errant like himself were the usual occupational hazards: wicked wizards, ogres, dragons, giants, enchantments. Perhaps a few lions or two. What bliss that life seemed to him now!

The pirates (if they were pirates, and none of the travelers could quite be sure) had abandoned the *Jolly Roger* with such alacrity that their passengers were left behind on the tilted deck. All of the longboats were gone, occupied by the crew; the ship listed again, sickeningly. She had probably ruptured her hull when she had run aground and was by now taking water at an alarming rate.

"Let's go ashore while we still have time to do so," advised Kesrick. He and Arimaspia clambered over the rail and he summoned the Hippogriff with a shrill whistle. The creature pricked up its ears and soared aloft, landing near where his master and mistress stood.

Mandricardo released his black charger from its cage, and he and Callipygia guided the horse down the slope of the deck. The two knights had to use their swords to chip away a section of the railing so that Bayardetto could get ashore.

They forgot the sacks of rubies in their haste.

"Certainly is a strange-looking place, what?" murmured the Tartar knight, staring around at what little could be discerned amid the clammy coils of the swirling fog.

And indeed it was. The shore was not sandy but seemed formed from solid rock. Everywhere, it was thickly encrusted with oysters and barnacles and thousands of seashells and pieces of driftwood. All of this was festooned with great clumps and masses of sour-smelling seaweed which resembled the slimy and tangled green beards of Tritons.

There were no trees to be seen, although the mysterious island seemed to be about an acre and a half in extent, and since they could only see part of it because of the pervading mist, they could not be sure of this.

They led the two beasts up to the rounded crest of the island, their boots and buskins squelching through the slippery weed, shells and barnacles crunching crisply underfoot.

Before they had gotten far up the slope, there sounded from behind them a groan of wrenching timbers and a raucous scraping sound; they turned to discover that the ship had slid off the shore and was some distance out to sea, proba-

The Mysterious Island

bly foundering and soon to go down. It vanished in the fog.

"Marooned," said Mandricardo cheerfully. Now that he stood on solid ground again, his spirits were beginning to perk up. And, after all, the voyage and the shipwreck were Adventures.

The women were shivering in the clammy fog, so Kesrick suggested they build a fire on the knoll, using the driest pieces of driftwood and clumps of weed they could find for fuel. In little time they had a small fire merrily blazing away. This warmed and cheered them all.

"How far are we from the seacoast of Bohemia, do you think, what?" inquired Mandricardo. Kesrick shrugged.

"We must have sailed several leagues by the time the *Jolly Roger* ran aground," he mused. "We still have a good ways to go."

"And no way to get there," remarked Callipygia. "You and your lady could fly to the coast astride Brigadore, of course. But Bayardetto can neither fly nor swim; Mandro and I are, as he said, marooned."

"Dear Cally, you know we would never abandon our comrades in peril," said Arimaspia.

"Certainly not," said Kesrick stoutly.

" 'Twould be against the jolly old Knightly Code, what," said Mandricardo. And he was right, of course: the Code was very strict on such situations.

"Perhaps," murmured Arimaspia—she always looked on the bright side of things—"perhaps with morning the fog will lift and some other ship will come by and rescue us."

"Perhaps," said Kesrick.

"Perhaps," echoed Mandricardo.

They had settled down for a nap beside the roaring fire, when quite suddenly and without the slightest advance warning, *the island moved beneath them.*

"Earthquake, by Jove!" exclaimed Sir Mandricardo, leaping to his feet in excitement.

But Kesrick shook his head doubtfully. It hadn't felt the same as an earthquake. It hadn't been quite like anything he could think of, except . . . you know how browsing cattle and horses twitch part of their hide to dislodge stinging flies? Well, it had been rather like that. And Kesrick pointed out this similarity to his companions.

"Goodness me," murmured Arimaspia, "I didn't know islands could *twitch!*"

"They can't, of course," said Kesrick briefly. "Therefore: either it wasn't a twitch, or—"

"Or this isn't really an island," said Callipygia.

They stared at each other blankly.

If they weren't on an island—what *were* they on?

"There it is again, dash it all!" exclaimed Mandricardo. And then another inexplicable phenomenon occurred.

"I say, old boy," remarked Mandricardo with a pretense of casualness, "I think the island is *moving.*"

They peered about, and saw that this was so. They could see the rocky shoreline *cutting through* the waves, for all the world like the prow of a boat.

The Mysterious Island

The same notion sprang into their minds simultaneously.

They were on the back of a sea-monster.

They looked at one another, round-eyed with dismay. It was not at all unlikely, of course, this being Terra Magica. After all, the same thing had happened to those dauntless mariners of ancient history, Sinbad of Basrah and Odysseus.

"Douse the fire," advised Kesrick. "The monster must have come to the surface, planning to drift idly and enjoy a nap; when we built a bonfire on its back, we must have awakened it."

"Mercy! *Look!*" quavered Arimaspia, pointing. The head of the monster was now visible, thrusting out into the churning waters like a blunt and rounded promontory. It was swimming for all it was worth, the island.

"Water—quickly!" said Kesrick. He feared the discomfort of having a bonfire built on his back would make the monster decide to submerge.

He and Mandricardo scooped up seawater in their helms and, before very long, they had put the blaze out, hoping that they had done it soon enough.

"After all, what, if the poor monster is irritated enough, it might decide to plunge to the bottom of the jolly old briny deep—taking us with it!" Mandricardo pointed out.

The unknown monster continued plowing through the waves, swimming steadily. Now that they were looking for it, they could see the huge flippers or paws that propelled the creature through the waves. It was neither an Orc, such as the one the Chevalier Rogero had once fought in order to rescue the Princess Angelica, nor the Leviathan on whose back Sinbad and his shipmates had once innocently camped. Kesrick decided, from the flinty composition of the island, their ship had run aground on Fastiticalon.

"On *who*?" asked Callipygia, wrinkling up her nose at the unfamiliar name.

"Fastiticalon, the gigantic sea-tortoise," Kesrick explained. "What we thought was a dome of rock is actually the carapace of the largest turtle in the world. Usually, I understand, he swims about down in the Erythraen Sea south of Taprobane."

"I say, that's the *fifth* one," murmured Mandricardo absently; between being shipwrecked and marooned, he was still trying to think of all of the Seven Seas.

4

Fat Man in a Boat

Gaglioffo clung whimpering to the iron rail of Zazamanc's flying chariot. Ahead, drawing the chariot through the skies as easily as a matched team of horses draws a light carriage down a country road, the hideous Wyverns flapped on furious wings. Perhaps they were happy to have been let out for a spree, or maybe they enjoyed the fact that the Paynim was not whipping them with an iron chain, as their former owner had frequently done. At any rate, they flew at a giddy pace through the night skies; already, they had crossed the burning waste and were now aloft above the moon-gilt waves of the Middle Sea, heading directly north.

Although he had flown before in this chariot, Gaglioffo had yet to become accustomed to flight. The sickening height, the giddy velocity, these affected him as much as the "bounding main" had disconcerted the gallant Sir Mandricardo. Therefore, he clung to the rail, eyes squeezed

shut, while wisps of damp cloud whipped by
and the sea swerved and swung horribly far
below.

After a while, the little Paynim unsqueezed
his eyes in order to ascertain how far they had
come thus far. And, as he did so, the dense fog
that mantled the waves far below parted suddenly to a vagrant breeze, and Gaglioffo espied
a ship drifting idly to the impulse of the tides.
From this height it looked more like a child's
toy than a real ship, but it was real enough, he
knew, and something impelled him to command the Wyverns to descend.

When they did, skimming above the masts,
Gaglioffo perceived, to his considerable puzzlement, that the vessel seemed completely deserted. All he could see on deck were the two fat
sacks of rubies that Kesrick and his friends had
inadvertently left behind.

He recognized them at once, and a gleam of
naked cupidity flared in his eyes. Ordering the
Wyverns to hover above the deck on throbbing
wings, the little Paynim scooped up the treasure and deposited it in the rear of the iron
chariot.

When at length he would arrive in the kingdoms of the West, at least he would not come
as a penniless wayfarer!

Fastiticalon continued on his (or her) voyage
across the Middle Sea, swimming at a pace no
oar-driven galley could possibly match. Still
were the waters fogbound and the visibility
thus diminished. All that the four travelers
could hope for, in their extremity, was that the

Fat Man in a Boat

monstrous sea-creature would decline to carry them to the oozy bottom of the sea, where the bones of drowned sailors lay amidst the rotting spars of sunken ships, great heaps of inestimable gems, and sea shells.

That the gigantic tortoise might actually bring them within wading-ashore distance of the Bohemian seacoast was, perchance, a bit too much to hope for.

After an hour or so, it seemed that Fastiticalon wearied, and decided to rest on the surface again—now that that bothersome bonfire was no longer blazing atop his shell. And the travelers looked at one another with a certain degree of relief, admixed with the trepidations only to be expected of mariners in peril.

Then—as things always seem to happen—there came a diversion of sorts. Out of the fog came a croaking voice which startled them.

"Avast, ye ninny! I said 'port' and 'port' I meant, ye scalpeen! Watch it, now, ye're about to run into something! Steady as ye go, bejabbers—"

And there emerged slowly out of the mist a peculiar vessel with an unusual crew of one. The boat was high-prowed as a Viking ship, but hardly bigger than a rowboat, with a square-rigged sail. Seated therein was a small fat man in monkish robes with a monkish tonsure. His face was round and red as an apple and in between croaking short-tempered remarks to his vessel, which seemed uncannily to steer itself, he swigged some potent liquor from a fat black bottle.

The queer little boat stopped dead of its own

accord, and the small fat man peered up at the bulk of Fastiticalon. Apparently, he spied the travelers camped on the upper part of the tortoise's shell, for he cupped the one hand that was not clutching the bottle about his lips and called out to them.

"Ahoy the monster! Faith, and ye seem to be ridin' about on a most unusual creeter! Be ye in need of rescue at all, at all?"

"We are indeed, kind and hospitable stranger," called out Arimaspia, since both knights were stricken speechless at this unexpected visitation. "But, alas, I fear your little boat is far too small to take us all aboard, including our noble steeds—"

"Little boat, is it, me lass! Faith, and Skidbladnir affords room enough fer yerself and all yer company," said the little fat man, exasperatedly. And then he addressed his self-propelled vessel in a language which none of them had ever heard.*

Whereupon the astonishing vessel stretched itself as a lazy cat does, elongating its prow, broadening its beam, and swelling its aft portions into more capacious accommodations. The ship seemed to do this all by itself and without aid from the little man in monkish robes, since he was gurgling down another swig of liquor from the fat black bottle at the time.

With alacrity, Kesrick and the others descended the slope of Fastiticalon's shell, leading their steeds, and gingerly climbed aboard Skidbladnir while the little man beamed at them

---

*I presume it was Gaelic. I've never heard it, either.

Fat Man in a Boat

complacently. Once they were all safely aboard, he addressed his vessel in stern tones.

"Now, be after payin' attention fer once, ye danged old ninny! Take us to the nearest land, which should be the seacoast o' Boheemy, and be quick about it, d'ye hear? No loiterin' on the way thither, or ye'll be after feelin' the back o' me hand!"

Obediently, the ship turned about and sailed off on a steady course into the boiling mist, leaving the monstrous turtle behind. The travelers, in unison, heaved a sigh of relief.

They felt it only fit and proper to introduce themselves to their eccentric little rescuer.

"I am hight Sir Mandricardo, son of King Agricane of Tartary, what?" said that worthy.

"How d'ye do, me b'y!"

"And I am hight Sir Kesrick of Dragonrouge," said the Frankish knight. They introduced the ladies.

"And what are you hight?" inquired Callipygia curiously.

"Well, as fer meself, me name's Colman Elo McBeosna Mac-ui-Seilli o' the Hy Neilles. St. Colman Elo Mac-ui-Seilli, by the bye," said the little man.

They were suitably impressed, none of them having ever met a saint before, such personages being about as rare in Terra Magica as they are in the Lands We Know. They had noticed a faint nimbus about his bald brows, but had been too polite to remark on it.

"An' as to how Oi come to be bobblin' about the high seas an' all," the Irish saint continued pleasantly, "well, Oi've always liked messin' about in boats and th' sea air's after bein' good fer me liver." He cleared his throat politely. "And, speaking o' livers, the ladies may be a might dampish, what with this filthy fog an' all; mayhap a wee drap o' poteen—jist to restore th' tissues?"

They passed the bottle about, taking each a gingerly sip of a fiery beverage stronger than raw brandy. (It may well have been whiskey, although it hadn't been invented yet.)

"Faith, an' there's no need for ye t' go so easy," said St. Colman *et al.* "Me bottle refills itself, y'see: a small miracle, but, what's the p'int o' bein' a saint, if ye can't work a miracle, now an' agin?"

"Very sensible point, begad," remarked Mandricardo, taking another swig.

"Oi've always loiked messin' about in boats, as I say," continued the saint, conversationally, taking another hefty swig of the beverage himself. "Ivver sinct me first voyage, when Oi braved the famous *coire Brecain* (ye Sassenacts w'd be after callin' it th' Whirlpool of Brecan; off the Isle of Rathlin it is, it is). Sometimes me voyages git confused wiv those o' me old pal and chum, St. Brendan, but there it is! And divil a bit it matters to the loikes o' me."

"It was indeed kind of your sanctity to rescue us from that dreadful monster," said Arimaspia respectfully. "May one inquire of your feast-day?"

"Ah, 'twas no trouble, lassie, no trouble at all! Fastiticalon's a dacent lad, take him all in all. For a turtle, that is! And very dacent o'e ye t' inquire after me feast-day; sure an' 'tis after

Fat Man in a Boat

bein' the twenty-sixth o' September. Come the next September twenty-sixth an' ye kin burn a candle or two in memory of our meetin', if ye loike."

Arimaspia promised to do so, even though she belonged to a different religion.

By this time, the sun was up and its rays had begun to dispel the cloak of mist. As the sea about them cleared, the travelers were relieved to see long combers pounding against a white strand, with green, forested hills rising beyond and mountains in the distance.

"Oh, I say! Jolly good," breathed Mandricardo; the pitching motion of the saint's magic boat had begun to upset him once again in the visceral regions.

"Here ye are, safe an' sound, high an' dry, jist as Oi promised," exclaimed the comical little Irishman. They disembarked, wading in the surf, leading their steeds up the stretch of sand, and bidding their saintly rescuer farewell and thanks.

"Not at all, not at all," he said amiably, waving away their words. "Happy to have been o' service t' ye all!"

Then he ordered Skidbladnir to turn about and the last they saw (or heard of him) was his hoarse voice admonishing the magic vessel sternly:

"Oi said 'turn about,' ye lazy scalpeen, an' about is what Oi mean! Git yer prow into th' wind, ye rascal, would ye be after embarrassin' me in front o' the foine gentry?"

5

The Man-Mountain

They found the beach deserted except for
themselves, with no signs of a town or city
nearby, and not even any fishermen. It was a
bright morning, the sky clear and pellucid, with
a brisk breeze blowing. They were all damp
and soggy from the sea voyage and the first
thing they desired was to get dry.

Kesrick and Mandricardo built a fire and
stretched out their cloaks on adjacent bushes.
While the two knights oiled their armor to pre-
vent rust, Callipygia unlimbered her bow and
strode off manfully into the fields. Since all
Amazons are excellent archers, and since she
was one of the several daughters of the present
Queen of Amazonia, it was not long before she
returned with a brace of plump pheasants, which
they quickly plucked, gutted and cooked.

His maritime adventures happily receding into
the past, the Tartar knight was quite restored to
his former good humor. While they munched

The Man-Mountian

on the steaming, delicious fowl and rested from their exertions during a long and mostly sleepless night, they conversed lazily.

"Dragonrouge lies north and west of here," said Kesrick. "But I'm not exactly sure precisely where 'here' is. Why don't we strike due north until we find a road and follow it to a town—since in my experience, roads generally lead *somewhere*—and then ask directions. I understand that the people in the Kingdom of Bohemia are a friendly and hospitable lot."

"Good-oh," nodded Mandricardo. "If that agrees with the ladies?"

It did.

"Pity we forgot to bring the rubies ashore," said the Tartar knight. "Haven't a spot of cash about me, I fear, so we'll have to trust to the hospitality of the Bohemians, what?"

Kesrick nodded. "I spent my last coin tipping the stableboy," he admitted. He looked at the women.

"Don't look at *me*, dear," said Arimaspia. Since she was quite naked, it was obvious that she had no more money on her person than she had raiment.

"I might have a pearl or two somewhere," said Callipygia, digging into the small leather pouch suspended from her girdle. As it turned out, she had three.

When they had finished their meal, they carefully extinguished the fire, donned dry clothing, mounted their steeds, and rode into the woods.

As the trees were rather widely spaced they were able to ride abreast, and to pass the tedium of the journey, they conversed.

41

"Once we have arrived at Dragonrouge," said Arimaspia, "you and dear Callipygia must stay with us awhile, sir knight."

"Jolly good!" nodded Mandricardo. "Have to be gettin' back to good old Tartary sooner or later, of course: the Pater must be perishing from curiosity as to what has befallen me. But it would be jolly to rest up for a time, after all these adventures and what-not. Huntin' any good in those parts, Sir Kesrick?"

"Quite decent, I think you'll agree," replied the Knight of Dragonrouge. "Usual stuff: bears, stags, boars, the occasional Ogre."

"Gettin' scarce, Ogres," commented Mandricardo. "Endangered species, what? Almost as rare as Dragons. Haven't broken a lance against a fairish Dragon since I was a lad. *Trolls*, now, that's another matter! Plenty of Trolls about."

Kesrick nodded. "Loads of 'em up north of Frankland, around the shores of the Frozen Sea. Might be able to scare up a wizard or two, or even a wicked enchanter for you . . ."

"No wizards, if you please," said Arimaspia determinedly. "That loathsome old Egyptian wizard was wizard enough for me, I assure you!"

"Witches, though," continued Sir Mandricardo with the true zest of a sportsman in his voice. "Witches are always fair game. Remember old Watzername, lived in the hut on chicken legs?"

"The one that melted when she got caught in the rain," nodded Kesrick, remembering very well their hair-raising adventure with Mother Gothel.

The Man-Mountain

They rode on at a leisurely pace, discussing sport.

Until Bayardetto stopped suddenly at the brink of an unexpected pit and nearly threw the Tartar knight and his Amazonian lady over the saddle-bow.

Brigadore the Hippogriff had spied the yawning hole in time to halt without endangering his riders. Arimaspia gasped.

"My goodness, are you two all right?"

"Tophole," declared Sir Mandricardo cheerfully. "Demmed inconvenient place to dig a hole, what? Ought to have it filled in; a felly could break a leg, comin' through the woods in the dark."

Kesrick said nothing, looking at the pit. It was about nine or ten paces in depth, shaped roughly like a kidney bean, and about twenty feet in length. A very odd sort of a pit, it seemed to him.

"Well, no bones broken. We can ride around the blasted thing, I suppose," said Mandricardo. He dismounted and led his black charger by his bridle into the bushes. Kesrick did the same on the other side of the peculiar pit.

They rode on at an easy pace. The forest was thinning out as they approached the hills. Several smallish mountains stood here and there about the landscape; in the distance, toward the east, a wide river glittered in the sunlight as it meandered between steep hills.

"That must be the Eridanus," he murmured half to himself.

"Probably," said Arimaspia, who had never heard of the river, being a stranger to these parts. She was busily drinking in the view, especially the hills and things. Her own country of Scythia was flat as a pancake, one endless prairie from border to border, and hills and mountains were still a novelty to her. They had rivers in Scythia, of couse, so she was less interested in *them*.

That mountain directly ahead was interesting, she thought. It seemed smaller and less wide than most—but the sun was in her eyes and she could not make it out with any clarity.

They came upon another one of those odd-shaped pits.

"King of Bohemia ought to have these holes filled in," Mandricardo grumbled. "Blighter can't expect to attract tourists to his country, if they're constantly falling in holes, what?"

They circumnavigated the second pit without difficulty, and found themselves on the edges of the forest. Ahead stretched a verdant plain, spotted here and there with more depressions that were probably much the same as the two pits. Kesrick thought it was all a bit strange, but nothing to *worry* about, surely.

Which proves that even the heroes of knightly romances can be dead wrong . . .

They emerged from the forest path in the open with Kesrick's Hippogriff in the lead. Arimaspia had just opened her mouth to ask a question about that oddly shaped smallish mountain directly ahead, when, and very suddenly, her breath left her in a gasp that sounded like a squeal of terror.

"Apia preserve us!" she squealed.

The Man-Mountian

For the mountain had just folded in the middle, and bent over, casting them in a deep shadow.

The very next instant a great hairy hand as large as a fourposter bed swooped down upon them. It was gnarled and callused, and the back of the hand and the knuckles bristled with hairs stiffer and thicker than broom-straws— almost like twigs.

Several things thereupon happened, virtually at the same time.

"Oh, jolly good—a giant!" exclaimed Mandricardo delightedly.

Then Bayardetto bucked and threw him and Callipygia out of the saddle, whereupon the horse prudently took to its heels. This was not cowardice on the destrier's part; not at all. Bayardetto was sensible enough to realize that there is hardly anything that a horse (even a war-horse) can do against a Giant.

At the same instant of time, the monstrous hand plucked both Kesrick and the Princess of Scythia out of their saddle and bore them aloft with sickening speed. It was like going up in an express elevator; this comparison did not, of course, occur to either Sir Kesrick nor his lady fair, as elevators were still unknown in Terra Magica.

The Hippogriff was affrighted, even as Bayardetto had been; the creature spread its wings and flew off, squawking shrilly.

Mandricardo and Callipygia watched it dwindle in the skies, heading due west.

BOOK TWO

KNIGHTS AND GIANTS

6

The Iron Castle

When Brigadore was frightened by having its two riders plucked out of the saddle by the hand of a Giant, and had taken wing in his fright, the Hippogriff had soared into the skies and had headed due west.

After a time, of course, the marvelous winged creature recovered from its panic, and began circling about. Sharp were the eyes of the hybrid griffin-horse—sharp as the eyes of hawk, falcon or eagle. But nowhere in the landscape below could Brigadore espy either his master and mistress or their companions.

Beneath him as he soared, riding the updraft on bronze-feathered wings strong and tireless, undulated a landscape of hills, forests, rivers, fields and farms, towns and cities. Nowhere did the Hippogriff see a familiar landmark.

But directly to the west of his present position there rose a mighty range of mountains that did seem familiar to the winged creature.

In lieu of any better idea, Brigadore swerved in his circling flight, and soared aloft toward that range of tall peaks.

Creatures of Brigadore's breed are accustomed to dwell in the mountains far to the north of the world. There, where a narrow strait connects the Caspian Sea with the Frozen Sea of the north, they nest and breed and raise their winged foals high atop the Rhiphaean Mountains, that march like a great boundary-wall between the western plains of Scythia and the mysterious Kingdom of the Hyperboreans.

But Brigadore had not been born on those lofty northern mountains, but far to the south, amid the Pyrénées. There dwells the famous magician, Atlantes, who breeds his herds of Hippogriffs as other men breed horses. And the mountains which Brigadore spied from afar, the mountains which had looked familiar to him, were in fact the Pyrénées.

Erelong the keen eyes of the Hippogriff recognized a flash of bright gray light from one of the loftier mountains. This was none other than the celebrated Iron Castle of Atlantes. Gratefully, the Hippogriff headed toward the only home he had ever known, and settled to earth before the stables where his fellow Hippogriffs were penned.

The amazing Iron Castle glittered and flashed and dazzled in the rays of the morning sun, but Brigadore gave the towers and battlements not a single glance. Unlatching the stable doors with his hooked beak, he stalked within, to croak greetings to his brothers and sisters and

The Iron Castle

aunts and uncles, and to drink from the trough set there for that purpose.

Then he settled down in the empty stall which had once been his, and patiently awaited the arrival of the servants of the Wizard of the Pyrénées, who would soon be entering the stables, yawning and scratching themselves, to feed the Hippogriffic herd, or flock, whichever may be the proper word.

Atlantes did not generally arise before ten o'clock in the morning, since old bones require rest, and his were already some centuries old. That particular morning, clad in his long nightshirt, a tasseled nightcap on his baldish head and his bony feet thrust into worn and comfortable carpet-slippers, he sat down at table and was served his favorite breakfast: a dish of hot oatmeal with plenty of milk and sugar, ripe oranges fetched by invisible spirits from the Hesperides, and strong tea laced with a jigger of brandy.

At about the midpoint of his repast, excited stablehands brought him the unexpected news of the arrival in the stables of *another* Hippogriff. One that should not be there at all, but who seemed perfectly at home.

"Wild or tame, would you say?" he inquired.

"One as is been already broke t' bit an' saddle, master," one of his hands replied. "In fac', already *wearin'* bit an' saddle. The critter also had this-here shield slung aboot its saddle-horn."

They displayed a shield familiar enough to Atlantes. It bore the heraldic emblem of Sir

Kesrick of Dragonrouge, to wit: *draco volans*, gules, on a gray field.*

" 'Pon my word!'' exclaimed the elderly sorcerer, tugging on his long white beard. "Whatever can have happened to that young felly?''

Hastily finishing his breakfast, Atlantes doffed his present attire and donned a long robe and sandals and strolled out to the stables in the back to investigate the matter himself. And, even as reported, he found a Hippogriff that was none other than Brigadore, peacefully enjoying his own breakfast, and recognized the Hippogriff from his markings, which were distinctive. Indeed, Brigadore recognized his former lord and master, too, and greeted him with a strange cry of welcome, halfway between a horse's neigh and the crowing caw of an eagle.

"Now, what on earth has happened to the young knight to whom I lent you at the behest of his fairy godmother, Pirouetta, the Fairy of the Fountain?'' mused Atlantes to himself in puzzled tones. "He was a polite and gentlemanly young fellow—for a Frank, that is—and I certainly hope no serious calamity has befallen him in the course of his adventures!''

Returning to his castle, the old magician entered his magical workshop and strove to discover the present whereabouts of Kesrick of Dragonrouge by means of his magic mirror,

---

*That is, a winged red dragon in flight on a gray background.

The Iron Castle

which was of polished black steel. Alas, he failed to find the Frankish knight.

"Well, then, *hrrumph!* I had best apprise Dame Pirouetta of these eventuations," said Atlantes to himself, and commanded the magic mirror to contact Kesrick's fairy godmother.

Unfortunately, this endeavor proved likewise fruitless; Dame Pirouetta's own magic looking-glass replied (civilly enough) that its mistress was absent on her sabbatical leave and was currently visiting the Mountains of the Moon, where she had relatives.*

Her looking-glass informed the Wizard of the Pyrénées that from this trip the fairy, who resided in an enchanted palace beneath a fountain in the midst of the forest of Broceliande, was not expected to return to her watery home until Tuesday next.

Leaving a brief message with the mirror so as to apprise Dame Pirouetta of the possible peril into which her favorite godson seemed to have fallen, Atlantes—who was a kindly and concerned old fellow, as magicians go—determined to look into the matter personally.

Donning his burnished steel armor, which was as bright as a mirror, putting on a visored helm and taking up his magical weapons, the very *least* of which were an enchanted sword and spear, he mounted on Brigadore and commanded the Hippogriff to seek out its master.

It had been the better part of a century since last Atlantes had left his celebrated Iron Castle

---

*And not the ones in North Africa, either: the ones on the Moon.

to go adventuring in the wide world, and the old fellow looked forward to the change with zest and gusto.

Gaglioffo, in the meanwhile, wearying of his giddy flight, had spotted a small town in Hyrcania and ordered the Wyvern-drawn chariot to earth behind a row of wooded hills. He then proceeded afoot into the town, found an inn, and ordered a huge breakfast for himself, which involved a slab of juicy steak, scrambled eggs, rashers of crisp bacon, hot fresh bread dripping with melted butter and swimming in honey, and a cup of hot chocolate.

The habitués of the inn eyed his sooty features, goggling eyes and blubbery lips with distaste, curiosity and suspicion. They were not accustomed to seeing Paynims nor Idolaters in these peaceful parts of their country, for, in fact, none had come hither since the mighty Emperor Charlemagne had driven back the Moors and Saracens some centuries before.

Still and all, for all that his appearance was repellent and his table manners despicable, they noted that Gaglioffo paid for his sumptuous repast with a glittering ruby as big as a baby's fist. Noting that, their suspicions were considerably allayed, and one or two of the townsfolk even voiced the hope that the bandy-legged little Paynim would stay awhile—presuming, of course, that he had more of those *lovely* rubies.

Nothing soothes the hostility of country people so much as the ostentatious display of good money.

Picking his teeth with a splinter, seated in

The Iron Castle

the courtyard of the inn under a blooming apple tree, Gaglioffo tried to decide what to do with himself next.

He had wealth and transportation at his disposal, but where would he be wisest to go? He had no friends or relations in these parts of the west, and in most of the kingdoms and countries where he did have acquaintances, at least, he was severely unwelcome. These countries included most of the Orient, for in his rather gaudy and criminous career, Gaglioffo had fled from quite a number of cities or countries about three steps ahead of the bailiff or sheriff.

With the contents of those two bulging sacks, the ugly little Paynim knew quite well he had riches which would suffice to keep him in comfort, if not in luxury, for the remainder of his natural life, however long that proved to be, and Gaglioffo intended it to be as long as he could manage.

The rubies would buy him a monarch's favor, perhaps even a dukedome of his own. Well, a fair-sized barony, at least. Paynim or no Paynim, money talks in Terra Magica as eloquently as it does here in Terra Cognita.

Putting his feet up and closing his eyes against the bright sunlight which struck through the boughs above his head, Gaglioffo decided to enjoy a late-morning nap before continuing upon his adventures.

He awoke to find a sword point at his throat and two yeomen busily attaching iron chains to his feet.

7

Thunderthighs

That very same morning, the Giant Thunderthighs woke somewhat earlier than did most of
the inhabitants of the west. The reason for this
was, that the Giant's perfectly enormous castle
rose atop the Alps and, as he slept in the topmost chamber of the tallest tower, the sun, as it
rose over the borders of the world in the regions of Far Cathay, shone through his bed-
room windows and aroused him from his rest
while most of Europe was still drowned in
darkness and fast asleep.

It had been quite some time since last the
Giant Thunderthighs had enjoyed a fish stew
for his dinner, so that morning he resolved to
go fishing. Yawning hugely*, and donning his
clothing, he slung his fishing line over one
shoulder and hung by its hook on his girdle a

---

*And when Giants yawn hugely, they yawn *hugely*.

Thunderthighs

small (small, that is, to him) iron-barred cage, in case smaller game chanced his way.

His fishing line was like the cable of a ship, and the fishhook he intended to use was larger than most ships' anchors.

Thus accoutered, he left his castle, closing and locking the front door thereof (although who would have the temerity to attempt to burgle the castle of a giant is more than I could guess) and descended the foothills of the Alps as you or I might descend a flight of steps, and set out for the sea.

An easy morning's amble took him the breadth of Europe. Arriving at the seacoast of Bohemia, his favorite fishing ground, he waded some distance out into the waters of the Middle Sea, but eventually became discouraged. There were no sea-monsters about that his rather weak eyes could discern—evidently, Fastiticalon had by this time sunk to the seabottom, or had swum off in the direction of the Nile or wherever.

Beginning his homeward amble, and having only picked up one small morsel to meaten his cookpot, he was pleased, while traversing the forests and fields of Bohemia, to discover two morsels more, which he plucked from the saddle of their strange steed and raised until they were at the level of his eyes.

He pondered them; and when Giants ponder, they ponder ponderously.

"Um! Little 'Uns! Tidbits fer me cookpot," he rumbled to himself, depositing the two tidbits carefully in the iron cage which hung at his girdle.

Then he continued on his journey across Europe.

While it is certainly a disconcerting experience to be plucked out of your saddle by the hand of a giant as tall as a four-story building, or nearly that, what is more disconcerting yet is to be raised to a level with the giant's face, while he squints rather near-sightedly at you.

Or so at least was the experience of the Scythian princess, Arimaspia, the heroine of this True and veritable History.

For one thing, she discovered that, when seen close up, the face of a giant is *extremely* unhandsome. You have to understand that both the Princess of Scythia and her Frankish knight were no longer than one of the giant's forefingers. You also have to understand that his beard and mane of hair were composed of strands thicker than rope, and so tangled and uncombed that they resembled nothing so much as thickets of thornbush.

Therein reposed dead leaves left over from the previous fall, and a number of birds' nests, some of them still affording a safe haven for nesting mother birds—safe even from hawks, which would have been to Thunderthighs only a minor and disagreeable annoyance, as mosquitoes are to such as you and I.

Moreover, the giant's face, seen this close, was repulsive. Down his narrow brow there trickled a drop of perspiration that could have filled a quart-bucket; the pores in his skin were so large that, had she wished for some reason to do so, Arimaspia could have put half the

Thunderthighs

length of one or even two of her fingers into one pore.

As he squinted at his two captives, pondering ponderously, the Scythian Princess was aware of a strange sound, rather like that caused by slowly-beaten drums. It took Arimaspia a few moments to understand that the sound she heard was caused by the pounding of the giant's pulse.

He was rather fat for a giant, with bowlegs, and his torso was clumsily clothed in coarse homespun cloth, out of which had been crudely fashioned a tunic and leggings. The weave of the cloth looked as if woven from ships' cordage, while his leggings were held together by strips of dragon-gut.

After pondering ponderously on the two—Sir Kesrick striving manfully all the time to free his arms from the rather loose but still unbreakable grip of the giant's fingers, in order to draw the deadly blade of Dastagerd, he placed them carefully in the iron cage that swung from his girdle, as I have said, and latching the top, set off for home.

The Giant Thunderthighs was about twenty times the height of a full-grown man, which is to say that he measured from heel to crown one hundred and twenty feet, more or less. Since his weight was in keeping with his height, Thunderthighs would have tipped the scales at something like four tons, had there been scales strong enough or large enough in that world to measure his weight. Now Kesrick understood those strange, kidney-shaped pits he and his companions had encountered in the forest, and into which they had almost fallen.

They were, of course, *footprints*.

Sir Kesrick was perfectly livid with fury: it is distinctly unheroic for the hero of a chivalric romance to be plucked out of the saddle as idly as you or I might pluck a mulberry from its bush. Wrapping his left arm around one of the bars which comprised their cage, he unlimbered the glittering blade of his enchanted sword, Dastagerd.

Then, looking down through the interlaced bars of the cage's floor, he paused to reconsider his next act. He had intended to hew through the iron bars with his enchanted sword—for that, after all, is what enchanted swords are *for*, to hew through that which is commonly unhewable. But . . .

Hanging as they were at the giant's waist, they were some sixty feet from the ground, and even if he freed them from this ignominious captivity, which was in itself quite humiliating, they could certainly be seriously injured by falling from this height to the ground. Especially, since the ground was moving rapidly beneath, such was the width of the giant's stride.

Even as Kesrick looked down and thought about it, Thunderthighs crossed a broad and rushing river that was probably the Eridanus as you or I might step easily across a trickle of water. He tramped along, flattening forests and crushing hills underfoot, at a pace so rapid that few horses could have kept up with his stride.

Kesrick changed his mind and put his sword away, rather shamefacedly. It was then that he

Thunderthighs

realized that he and his princess had a companion in their misery; that is, another person shared the cage with them.

This was a young man with a long, woeful face, dressed in a surcoat over a long suit of mail, as was Kesrick. He had, however, neither helm nor sword nor shield (and it was not until that moment that the Knight of Dragonrouge remembered that he had left his own shield, charged with the blazonry of Dragonrouge, looped by a leathern thong over the saddle-bow of Brigadore).

"Sir knight, I am hight Sir Kesrick of Dragonrouge, a knight of the Franks, and this is my lady-love, the Princess Arimaspia of the Scythians," he introduced himself with chivalric courtesy.

The sad-faced young man replied in similar fashion.

"I am hight Sir Felixmarte of Hyrcania, and my own true lady-love is the misfortunate Lady Lunetta, the Princess of Bohemia," he declared in hollow and dolorous tones. "I was seized from the saddle of my destrier in mid-morn by this dastardly giant, as I traced the plain hoping to free my beloved, the Princess Lunetta, from a vile and villainous enchantment. I left my sword and spear, and helm and shield behind, I'm afraid," he added gloomily.

"Nothing to fret about; happens all the time," declaimed Kesrick, striving to cheer the fellow up.

"Pray tell us, Sir Felixmarte, if you can, where this hideous monster is taking us, and what, in your estimate of the situation, he intends to do with us," Arimaspia inquired.

The Hyrcanian knight saluted her dispiritedly.

"He is the Giant Thunderthighs, according to the histories of famous giants I have studied; *de venere Golidad*—of the lineage of Goliath—and a distant cousin of the notorious Blunderbore," said Felixmarte.

"Oh," remarked Arimaspia in a small voice.

"And as for what the monster's intentions toward us are, I hesitate to say, madame, but I greatly fear they include luncheon. That is, the mention of *the cookpot* has recently been made within my hearing."

"Oh," said Arimaspia again, and this time even more faintly.

"Um," said Kesrick, unhappily. Now he understood why Sir Felixmarte of Hyrcania looked sad and gloomy.

Nobody likes to be thought of as lunch.

8

Rewards of Villainy

When Bayardetto, affrighted by the giant, bucked and threw his riders, both landed unhurt, their fall cushioned by the thick lushness of the meadow grass. Sir Mandricardo, however, landed flat on his back and the impact jolted the wind out of him. It took him some moments to get his breath back.

Callipygia helped him to his feet again: Mandricardo looked around, swearing by his halidom and other knightly curses. His destrier was still in full flight, so there was nothing to do but to go charging after Thunderthighs afoot, which he did. Drawing his sword and yelling challenges at the top of his voice, he began chasing the giant, with the Amazon girl at his side.

This soon proved to be a hopeless proposition. Since the Giant took about thirty paces at an easy stride, he could cover a lot more ground than could Mandricardo and Callipygia, and in much less time.

Within two minutes or less, the Giant had covered half a mile, and Mandricardo, puffing along in pursuit, realized the hopelessness of trying to overtake the monster on foot, encumbered as he was by the weight of his weapons and his mail. Armor was never meant to be worn while running.

By the time they had reached the shores of the Eridanus—which Thunderthighs stepped over easily—Mandricardo was exhausted. He stood there, knee-deep in the rushes which grew thick along the riverbank, fuming, waving his sword and yelling things like: "Come back here and fight like a man, you monster, what?"

It did no good. If Thunderthighs heard him at all, he probably mistook the far, faint noise for the humming of a bee. With stride after ponderous and space-eating stride, the giant receded into the distance.

The Tartar knight sat down on a boulder, digging the point of his sword into the earth moodily, and muttering oaths to himself, presumably in Tartar. Callipygia tried to be helpful.

"Yon river's not too wide. Perchance we could swim across?" she suggested.

"We'd have to leave our weapons and armor behind, dash it all," groaned Mandricardo. It was a good point, surely. He refrained from mentioning that he couldn't swim, there being few lakes or rivers on the steppes of Tartary.

" 'Twould not be knightly or honorable to abandon our companions to their peril," the Amazon girl pointed out. This stung Sir Mandricardo. The very thought of Sir Kesrick and

Rewards of Villainy

the Princess Arimaspia serving as the main course in the Giant's lunch tormented him. He growled something under his breath—either a prayer or a curse—in a tongue unknown to the Amazon girl.

However, he didn't move from the boulder whereon he sat with his shoulders slumped. Callipygia became a little sharp-tempered.

"Tirante the white would not have given up. Neither would the gallant Palmerin," snapped Callipygia, primly. "Indeed, if I recall my history, under similar circumstances, the noble-hearted Esplandian—"

"Dash it all, m'dear, what d'you expect me to do? *Fly* across this bloody river?" said Mandricardo rather rudely. His ladylove gave him a Look.

"What I expect my brave chevalier to do," she said between her teeth, "is to stop sitting there like a great ninny, and get on his hind legs and help me find a stretch of shallows, where we can *ford* this filthy stream!"

The Tartar knight flushed crimson—what with his swarthy complexion. Callipygia was, of course, right. He got to his feet, and gave her a hug, wordless but in itself eloquent.

They took opposite directions along the riverbank, with Sir Mandricardo going north and the Amazon girl heading south.

Bayardetto recovered from his panicky giant-fright at about the same time as had Brigadore. The difference was that, lacking the wings to fly, the black charger had not gone as far in the same time as had the Hippogriff, and had not gotten lost. Pausing to snatch a prudent mouthful or two of meadow-grass, he soon came trotting back in the direction in which he had fled. Neither of his two riders were any longer in view, but once a war-horse, always a war-horse.

He followed Mandricardo's footprints, and soon caught up with him, whinnying with eagerness and asking forgiveness for his quite un-war-horselike behavior in the face of the enemy.

Mandricardo was not a man to hold a grudge for long. Thumping the strong shoulders of his steed with the flat of his hand and stroking his satiny muzzle, he gruffly said soothing things like: "There, there; no harm done, what?"

Shortly thereafter, Mandricardo heard the faint halloo of a hunting horn to the south. As this was the signal they had both agreed upon, should either of them succeed in locating a ford, he knew thereby that Callipygia had found one. He mounted his steed and went pricking off across the plain.

Gaglioffo raised a wailing cry, calling upon the several Idols of his Paynim kind, and begging to know what he had done to deserve such treatment.

The man who held his sword-point to his captive's throat was stout, bluff and hearty, red-faced, with steely eyes. He was, it eventuated, the constable in charge of keeping the King's Peace in this village, and was not about to permit any rascally malefactors to avoid the clutches of justice.

"Yer monster-drawn chariot beyond them hills," said this worthy in gruff, accusing tones, "done et up three geese from th' flock. Goosegirl

Rewards of Villainy

tending 'em ran to swear out a complaint against yer."

Gaglioffo rolled his eyes in relief. So minor an offense could easily be remedied: one of the smaller of the many rubies in the treasure-sacks should afford a recompense more than sufficient . . .

"Gladly will I make full and generous restitution to the poor wench, by Mahoum!" he swore feelingly. "My funds are prudently concealed from obvious view in the rear of my vehicle . . ."

His voice stilled. There was something in the eyes of the stern, fat constable that gave him forebodings.

"Aye, ye rascal, we found yer sacks," grunted the officer. "The King o' Scythier reported 'em stolen some time back. Seems he offered a hefty ransom fer th' return of his dotter, or her rescue from some monster er other, I fergit which—and a foreign scoundrel sech as yerself made off wif 'em. Never did git th' gel back, poor soul."

"But—!"

The constable held up one of the sacks, pointing to the painted heraldic emblem thereupon. It represented a Catobleps quartered with three Gryphons, the Royal Arms of Scythia, and above it was written *Royal Scythian Treasury, #42, 697.*

The ugly little Paynim groaned pitifully. He could see no way out of this dilemma.

"Aye, we got yer dead t' rights, ye rascal!" growled the constable in high satisfaction. "Yer loot is confiscated, an' yer sorcerous chariot'll be held as evvydince against yer."

Rewards of Villainy

"But, your worship, I—I—" wailed Gaglioffo. The constable, however, was paying no attention, busily scribbling figures on the back of a bit of paper.

"Stealin' fum foreign monarchs: thet's good fer a month in pokey right thar," he muttered. "Frightenin' pore li'l goosegirls: three, four days. Drivin' monsters about th' Kingdom: two weeks, mebbe more. Lettin' 'em eat geese as belongs t' other folks: two days per goose. Thet's seven weeks, right thar." He looked up, bending a severe look of reproof on the trembling Paynim. "Oh, we do be law-abidin' folks up here in Hyrcanier, me bucko, you kin count on thet!" He nodded to the yeomen. "Take 'im away, boys. We'll let th' rogue cool 'is heels in gaol until the magystrate gits back from 'is fishin'-trip."

"Wh-when will that be, O Fountain of Hospitality?" whimpered the Paynim fearfully.

The constable shrugged carelessly.

"The way them trout be leapin,' say six er sivven weeks. Mebbe more. Do yer duty, boys."

They led the hapless Gaglioffo off in chains, to share a miserable straw pallet in a stone cell with several families of lice, and to strive to beat the rats to his dinner, which consisted of a mouldy crust of bread or two and a tin dish of water.

Thus (solemnly comments the True and Veritable History of the Knight of Dragonrouge at this point) are the rewards of villainy.

The Wizard of the Pyrénées soared through the noonday skies, mounted in the saddle, which was strapped between the powerful bronze-

Rewards of Villainy

feathered, gold-tipped wings of the Hippogriff. He had already traversed the southern parts of the famous Kingdom of the Franks, to say nothing of Bohemia and several other smaller and less important countries.

Atlantes was enjoying himself mightily. It had been many years, as I remarked earlier in this narrative, since the magician had found the occasion to leave his celebrated Iron Castle atop the mountain peak, for he was of scholarly and studious mind, and enjoyed his sedentary life, pondering sorcerous tomes and mucking about with spells and philtres and incantations and what-not.

He had given Brigadore his head, and had ordered the beast to find his master; thereafter, Atlantes simply sat back in the saddle and relished the view, which, from this height, was quite spectacular.

Along toward early afternoon, Brigadore suddenly pricked up his ears and uttered an excited, neighing cry. It was obvious to one as perceptive as Atlantes, that the Hippogriff had spotted something far below that seemed familiar to him. He tossed the reins loosely in a signal to descend, and as the great Hippogriff began circling down through the sky—for all the world like a hawk lazily descending upon a plump rabbit—the magician leaned over the side and peered curiously down to see what Brigadore had discovered.

The rushing wind made his eyes water, but even so Atlantes could see that Sir Kesrick was not in view, and he frowned with puzzlement . . .

9

The Giant's House

As the Giant Thunderthighs proceeded across Europe into the east at an easy, ambling stride, the tidbits he had found to sweeten his cookpot swung giddily in the iron cage at his girdle.

The only way to keep from being tossed about, as Sir Felixmarte explained, was to hang on with both hands to the bars of the cage and to brace your feet. Otherwise, with every stride, the giant would have slammed them about against the sides of the cage, which would have bruised Sir Kesrick and the Scythian princess severely.

Especially the princess.

Hanging on with both hands and trying not to get banged about, Kesrick could not get to the enchanted sword Dastagerd. And since they were a good sixty feet off the ground, he would not have cut through the bars, even had he been able to. The only thing to do was to reach their des-

The Giant's House

tination—whatever it might be— and hope that the giant would put the cage down.

Biding his time and hoping for the best, Kesrick tried to estimate the speed at which the Giant Thunderthighs was traveling. At thirty paces per stride, and considering that he had been strolling along now for about half an hour ... well, Sir Kesrick's mastery of elemental arithmetic was perhaps not all that it could have been; but he believed they had come about ten miles by this time.

Ten miles in half an hour is faster than any war-horse could have traveled, and longer than any horse known to the Knight of Dragonrouge could have maintained so rapid a pace.

His heart sank within him. It had, of course, occurred to the young Frank that Mandricardo and the Amazon girl would be hot on their trail, and with a trail so clearly marked—for with every step, the giant left a footprint twenty feet long and impressed some six or nine feet into the soil, depending, of course, upon the terrain—it would have been a remarkably easy trail to follow.

But even Bayardetto, strong of wind and fleet of foot as he was, could not have run ten miles in thirty minutes, encumbered with two riders in armor, and if their former comrades were riding in pursuit, by now they must have gotten far behind. Kesrick set his jaw grimly: he could not count on others to rescue him and his lady-love, but only on himself.

And, of course, on the long-faced knight who shared the cage with them. He seemed a fit-enough fellow, for all his sad looks and hopeless love for his enchanted Princess. Kesrick opened his mouth to ask about the enchantment in question, but, just then, Thunderthighs swerved to one side in order to avoid a medium-sized mountain, and Kesrick was slammed against the side of the cage, which knocked the breath out of him and bruised a few ribs.

He decided to save his breath for hanging on, and to leave the questions until later.

By about six o'clock in the evening, having traversed roughly one hundred and twenty miles, by Kesrick's rude estimate, the giant arrived at the Upper Alps, which he proceeded to climb from foothills to higher foothills, as we would ascend a flight of steps.

The giant's castle was every bit as huge as you might expect the castle of a giant to be. With the exception of the enchanted palace of the genie Azraq, which Kesrick and Arimaspia had visited on an earlier adventure,* it was the tallest structure that either the Frankish knight or his lady-love had ever seen. With the possible exception of the celebrated Tower of Babel, which was still standing in this day and age, although in a state of considerable dilapidation, it might well have been the tallest building in all of Terra Magica.

Thunderthighs unlatched his front door and went in. His living room was larger than Mammoth Cave (which hadn't been discovered yet), and the ceiling was higher than the roof of any cathedral yet constructed. Unhooking the

*See my novel *Kesrick* to which *Dragonrouge* is the sequel.

The Giant's House

iron cage from his belt, the giant set it down atop his dinner table, which would have dwarfed most of the mesas in Arizona, hung his fish-line and hook on a peg behind the door, and prepared to cook dinner.

He took up an iron cauldron larger than quite a few lakes and filled it from the waterfall in his backyard, using about fifteen thousand gallons for the purpose. Then he hung it on an iron hook, lit a fire in the grate (employing about half of the tree trunks in a medium-sized forest for kindling), and began preparing his meal.

He tossed into the pot about four wagon-loads of turnips, to which he was partial, two wagon-loads of carrots, another two of potatoes, and half a ton of onions. He then salted and peppered the beginnings of his stew with a sufficiency of those condiments to have supplied a regimental mess for a solid year.

He had invited to dinner a day or two before, one of his neighbors, the Giant Stumbleduffer, who lived a league or two up north, on the borders between Orn and Puffleburg. But he didn't expect Stumbleduffer to arrive for at least an hour and a half, so, in the meanwhile, tuckered out by his exertions of the day, Thunderthighs decided to take a nap.

Leaning back in his chair, lacing his hands together over his enormous paunch, he nodded off and soon began snoring. It was an unnerving sound, so deep in timbre as to make Arimaspia's teeth ache.

"Now's our chance to escape," whispered Kesrick—although even he could not have explained why he was whispering, since nothing of lower decibels than a major thunderstorm or perhaps a volcanic eruption, would likely have roused the giant from his rest.

Requesting Arimaspia and Sir Felixmarte to stand out of his way, Kesrick unlimbered Dastagerd and began hewing lustily at the iron bars of their cage. At each blow, the bars rang like a gong, but Kesrick could not help that, and, anyway, he doubted if Thunderthighs could hear it over the deep thunder of his own snoring.

Arimaspia was gazing around at the giant's table with awe and a certain childish delight. It was set with teacups bigger than carriages, and bowls that would have made excellent swimming pools, and set with knives longer than boar-spears and spoons the size of shovels. Not to mention the forks, which would have made good pitchforks for farmers pitching hay.

The salt and pepper shakers were slightly taller than a grown man.

It took the perspiring Sir Kesrick all of ten minutes to cut through the iron bars in order to make an opening large enough for the three of them to squeeze through. Then he and Felixmarte of Hyrcania put their shoulders to the task of bending the stumps of the severed bars out of the way. Once the opening was deemed large enough to their judicious gaze, Kesrick stepped out upon the table first and gallantly offered Arimaspia his hand, with Sir Felixmarte the last to emerge from the cage.

They ventured across the plateau-like table-

The Giant's House

top to its edge, which took some little time, and peered down.

"Goodness, how ever are we going to get down?" breathed the Scythian princess. Sir Felixmarte looked even glummer than was normal for him; Arimaspia was right—they were a good fifty feet from the floor. To jump from this height would surely pulverizre every bone in their bodies.

"We might cut steps down one of the table-legs," muttered Kesrick, half to himself. But even he thought that was risky. For one thing, there wasn't much to hold onto; for another, it would surely take too long.

Already the fifteen thousand gallons of water in the giant's cookpot were beginning to simmer, filling the enormous room with the delicious odor of boiling vegetables. Since none of them had eaten a bite since breakfast, the delectable aroma made their mouths water.

They discussed various notions as to how they could descend from the huge table, at length deciding on a desperate chance. The giant's legs were spread and his jerkin was stretched from knee to knee, like a trampoline, albeit a very large one. As the giant's lap was not all *that* far beneath them, Kesrick determined that they should jump one by one into Thunderthigh's lap, and then clamber down his leggings to the floor.

He went first, landing easily enough, and climbed up the coarse-woven garment to the Giant's knee. Arimaspia followed, also without harm, and then came Felixmarte, who botched the jump and nearly, but not quite, landed on the floor.

The Giant grumbled a time or two, in between his snores, but did not awaken.

They climbed down Thunderthigh's leggings, finding it no more difficult than to descend a rope-ladder, and avoiding his feet (which were bare in sandals, and might have been sensitive enough to arouse him, had they walked across them), jumped down to the floor from the height of his ankles, a mere sixty inches, or so.

"Where now, sir knight?" Felixmarte panted. Kesrick had more or less taken command by now, and all of his ideas had proven to be good ones. The young Frank pointed.

"The front door," he advised. "There's a crack beneath it, of course: there always is. It may be only an inch or so to *him*, but it may be enough for folks of our size to crawl under."

Without further discussion, the three headed off in the door's direction. In order to reach it they must traverse a seemingly illimitable plain of floor, but they had no other recourse.

It seemed to the adventurers that it took them an hour or more to cross that flat, endless prairie of flooring, but eventually it was accomplished and they arrived at the colossal portal, panting for breath and winded from their exertions.

Despite their desperate straits, Arimaspia giggled and pointed.

There was a mousetrap behind the giant's door, big enough to snap a grizzly's spine.

"I wonder what sort of *mice* a giant's bothered by," she said, smiling.

The Giant's House

"Maybe it's a beartrap," muttered Kesrick urgently. "Come on!"

They got flat on their bellies and were about to attempt to crawl under the door (which loomed above them like a flat Matterhorn of wood), when suddenly it shook to a thunderous pounding that sounded not unlike a bombardment of artillery.

Felixmarte groaned feelingly, and paled, rolling up his eyes.

It could only be the knuckles of the Giant Stumbleduffer pounding on the door.

He had come to share his neighbor's dinner.

To which they were intended to be at least the hors d'oeuvres!

10

Joining Forces

From aloft, the Hippogriff's keen eyes had discerned and recognized the forms of Mandricardo the Callipygia, mounted upon the black
charger, Bayardetto. Knowing them to be the
friends and companions of his master, the creature had sounded its call, and now made a
swooping descent, landing neatly directly in
their path and making the destrier, a trifle ner-
vous ever since the advent of that *giant*, swerve
suddenly.

By this time in the afternoon, the three had
forded the river Eridanus at the safe crossing
the Amazon girl had discovered, and were rapidly traveling east in the direction in which
Thunderthighs had carried off Sir Kesrick and
the Princess of Scythia.

There was no danger of losing the trail—not
when you were following footprints six feet
deep every thirty paces or so.

Sir Mandricardo was about to shout his

Joining Forces

knightly challenge and offer battle to the intruder, when, somewhat nonplussed, he recognized Brigadore. He hadn't seen too many Hippogriffs but it was Brigadore's distinctive gold-laced bridle that enabled him to identify the steed of his friend.

"Pray put up your sword, sir knight," said Atlantes. "I am no foe, but a friend to yourself and Sir Kesrick. My name is Atlantes—"

The eyes of the Tartar knight sparkled with enthusiasm; from boyhood, he had reveled in histories of chivalry and knightly derring-do, which explains why, Tartar or no Tartar, he had modeled himself upon his heroes.

"I say, dash it all, not the famous Wizard of the Pyrénées!" he exclaimed.

Atlantes preened his long white beard with one skinny hand.

"The very same," he said modestly.

"Oh, good-oh! We could use a friendly magician at this point, what? This is H.R.H. the Princess Callipygia, daughter of the Queen of the Amazons, you know."

"Delighted to make your acquaintance, madame," said Atlantes with a courtly nod.

They dismounted, and while their steeds rested and fed, they discussed recent events. Atlantes was distressed to learn that Sir Kesrick had been carried off by a giant—and explained how Brigadore had flown back to his own stall in the stables of the famous Iron Castle atop the Pyrénées.

"We've been following the blighter's trail all afternoon," said Mandricardo, finishing up his brief account of their perils and travails, "but when we can hope to catch up with him is anybody's guess," said Mandricardo gloomily.

"Perhaps we had best join forces in order to effect the rescue of the young felly," suggested Atlantes affably. "Of course, the problem is that Brigadore can travel farther, and very much faster, than can your noble destrier, lacking wings."

"I say, you're a magician, what?" exclaimed Mandricardo. "Why not use your powers to put wings on my Bayardetto?"

The Wizard of the Pyrénées considered the notion for a moment or two, then reluctantly shook his head.

"It's not all that simple, sir knight," he confessed. "Oh, I suppose I could do it, yes; but Bayardetto would have had to have had wings ever since he was foaled, in order to know how to fly. Takes time, you know; not learned in a day, flying. Even Hippogriffs like Brigadore here have to be pushed off a precipice, sometimes, in order to learn how to use their wings."

"Bloody rotten luck," remarked Mandricardo. They continued the discussion, arguing alternative plans.

While the conversation was taking place, Callipygia the Amazon was studying the Wizard of the Pyrénées with bright eyes. He was tall and lean and lanky, with a thrusting beak of a nose and a long white beard, his skinny frame clad in mirror-bright plate armor designed in a fashion that had gone out of style a century ago or more.

He quite reminded her of the enchanter

Joining Forces

Osmund whom she had encountered on one of her own adventures, which had taken place some time before she ever met Mandricardo or Kesrick or Arimaspia and became involved in their journeys and adventures. She was tempted to ask Atlantes if he happened to be any relation to her enchanter foe, but decided not to, since time was passing on at its inexorable pace, and the sun was declining steadily in the west. Soon would come twilight, and the cook-pot would be on the fire . . .*

It was eventually decided that Atlantes, mounted on the Hippogriff, would fly ahead to scout out the terrain, and that when he finally spotted a Giant's castle, he would return to apprise Sir Mandricardo and his Amazonian sweetheart of the precise direction and distance.

Saluting the two, he remounted Brigadore and soared off into the east, following the trail of enormous footprints.

Dame Pirouetta, the Fairy of the Fountain, returned from the Moon somewhat earlier than she had anticipated. She had enjoyed her visit with her second-cousin twice-removed, the Fairy Blackstick, but her other relatives had proven a boring lot, and when you have seen one Moun-

---

*I consider it a real misfortune for my readers that this early adventure of Callipygia and the enchanter Osmund cannot be given here. It would be a serious digression and would impair the smooth and mellifluous flow of this narrative. But it was a thrilling episode in her career—involving her enchantment into a cactus-plant, two ogres, and the intervention of a Good Fairy—and would certainly make exhilarating reading.

tain of the Moon, you have seen them all, at least in her opinion.

Beneath the bubbling waters of the enchanted pool amidst the magical and mysterious forest of Broceliande, she entered her palace and promptly began scolding the nixes who were her servants for their lackadaisical ways.

"Look at that sideboard, I ask you!" she snapped. "Dust an inch thick! And the highboy! And who has been washing my best crystal and leaving these dreadful spots upon every piece! I only hope my cut-glass has received better care, but I perceive it has not—!"

With these domestic criticisms to be made, and the drapes taken down for the laundry, and a spot or two (or three) to be carefully removed from her Persian carpets, it took most of the morning before Kesrick's fairy godmother got around to consulting whatever messages might have been received by her magic looking glass* during her absence.

The urgent message left by Atlantes, of course, was uppermost in her concerns. Of all the thirty-seven princes, knights or princesses to whom she performed the tasks of being fairy godmother, the young knight of Dragonrouge was her especial favorite, and ere this she had helped him out of more than a few tight spots.

One of the nixes came timidly into her mistress' dressing-room.

"Madame, we have laundered the drapes and dusted and waxed the highboy and the side-

---

Which apparently serves as Terra Magica's version of the telephone answering service.

Joining Forces

board, as you ordered. Undina wishes to know whether or not you want us to repolish *all* of the silver—"

"I've no time for such trivial matters now!" snapped Dame Pirouetta, snatching her second-best fairy wand off the rack. "Order my Cloud immediately!"

The pounding on his front door was loud enough to arouse Thunderthighs from his nap, and he unlatched the door and opened it to admit his guest, the only other Giant who lived in the neighborhood.

Stumbleduffer proved to be about as tall as Thunderthighs, but thinner, somewhat more kempt in appearance, and amiable in temperament. The two shook hands and exchanged greetings in low, rumbling tones like rolls of thunder.

Giving his guest a chair, Thunderthighs ambled over to inspect the monstrous cauldron, finding it boiling merrily by now and filling the enormous room with appetizing and mouth-watering odors. Returning to the table to pop into the boiling brew the morsels he had found that morning, he was dismayed to discover the ingenious tiny creatures had somehow managed to escape.

Rumbling a brief apology to his guest, Thunderthighs went out on the front stoop and scanned the slopes of his Alp in every direction. Night had fallen, or was just about to, and the light was much too dim for his weak eyes to make out anything that looked like escaping Little 'Uns. He was tempted to take up his club, which was fashioned from the entire length of a thousand-year-old California redwood, and go after them, *fee fi fo fum*ing in the approved giantly tradition*, but thought better of it.

The reason for this may take a bit of explaining, so bear with me. It seems that, in Sir Kesrick's day and age, it was considered quite *déclassé* for giants to devour ordinary-sized mortals, either raw or cooked. Indeed, among the better class of giant society it was thought (if you will pardon the pun) *rather in bad taste.*

Now Thunderthighs' guest, the Giant Stumbleduffer, was among those giants too genteel to eat men. Not that Stumbleduffer was a vegetarian; quite the contrary, he had no objections at all to a herd of roast cows, or a broiled brace of buffalo, or a few slabs of elephant steak, and was, in fact, particularly fond of fillet of whale (which is partly why Thunderthighs had gone fishing that morning).

But Man was simply *not eaten* by giants of the better sort.

So, rather than admit that he had planned to slip two or three Little 'Uns into the vegetable stew, in lieu of anything larger or tastier, Thunderthighs avoided the matter and served the stew to his guest. After all, there were loaves of brown bread to eat with the hot stew (they were the shape, and very nearly the size, of locomotive engines), drenched in enough melted butter to have easily drowned a few Bengal

---

Giants have rather poor eyesight, but they can sniff out Man better than bloodhounds.

Joining Forces

tigers, so it was not that there was too little to put on the table.

This meal they washed down with hogsheads of brown ale, each of which they emptied at a gulp. And, after their supper, the two giants stoked their pipes and played a friendly game of cards. Their cards, incidentally, were about the size of bedsheets. Then they called it a night.

Kesrick, Arimaspia and Sir Felixmarte were nearly down the mountain by this time, having crawled under the door when Thunderthighs closed it behind his guest.

BOOK THREE

ESCAPING THE COOK-POT

11

A Hospitable Friar

Gaglioffo languished in durance vile for a full day and part of the night, calling upon his favorite idols Mahoum and Termagant, and so on. Then he stopped relying upon supernatural aid and began to use his own wits.

They had thrust him into one of the cells on the ground floor of the gaol, and the wyverns (as he discovered by peering out of the small barred window that overlooked the courtyard of the gaol) were penned in the stables, held as evidence against him. Having filled their bellies on the goosegirl's flock of geese, the ugly reptiles were somnolent. But they were not out of earshot.

The bandy-legged little Paynim cleverly waited until nightfall, when even the constable was asleep and snoring at his desk in the front office. Then he unlimbered the small silver whistle by which his late master, the Egyptian wizard Zazamanc, had summoned and commanded the scaly brutes.

Now Gaglioffo had been in gaols before, many of them, in fact: some better and more comfortable than this, quite a few less snug and cozy. On the whole, however, he was heartily sick of gaols and would very much prefer never to see the inside of one again. A sentiment with which, I am sure, all of my readers would agree.

Therefore, once night had fallen and the constable was snoring noisily in the office, he tiptoed to the little barred window and summoned the wyverns by tootling (as softly as he could manage) on the little silver whistle.

Ears pricked to the alert, the wyverns came slithering to the window, dragging the iron chariot with them, and shattering the wooden fence about the stable in their progress. The Paynim then ordered them to set him free.

Now the saw-toothed beaks of Wyverns are harder than iron, harder even than decent steel—almost as hard as adamant itself, in fact. Therefore, it did not take them very long to bite through the bars of the window, which were of soft iron.

Huffing and puffing, panting and wriggling, Gaglioffo squeezed his bulk through the small window, to gingerly pat the hissing reptiles on their scaly heads. Then he led them around to the other side of the gaol, where another small barred window gave forth upon a view of the alleyway from the second cell, where the twin sacks of rubies reposed, safely under lock and key, in case the temptation of such wealth might

A Hospitable Friar

tend to swerve one or another of the townsfolk from the strict path of law-abidingness.

It took the two Wyverns no longer to bite asunder and to pry apart the bars of the second window than it had taken them to serve the first. Gaglioffo then reached in and hauled out the two sacks of rubies.

Only then did the Paynim relax with a *whoosh* of relief, and fan his fevered brow, knees rubbery and hands shaky from the tension—although this was not, by far, the first gaol he had ever broken out of.

However, he resolved that it was the *last*.

Flinging the twin sacks to the rear of the iron chariot, he mounted the vehicle and tootled on the silver whistle. The wyverns spread their bat-ribbed wings (exuding a curious stench that was partly the sour smell of a snake's-nest, intermixed with a burning stench of sulfur and, of course, brimstone) and flapped up into the air, narrowly missing a rooftop or two in the ascent.

Now, the question was—where or whence or whither to fly?

They loved him not in Basrah. In Baghdad, the Caliph's court held him in bad repute. There were warrants out for his arrest in Scythia. Posters with his likeness were pasted upon the walls of Samarkand and the principal cities of Far Cathay. There were Rajahs down in Hindoostan who dreamed almost nightly of him, and those dreams included interesting punishments like boiling oil and being buried up to the earlobes in a giant nest of red ants.

He was most particularly unwelcome in the

country of the Hyperboreans, in which country, and for what seemed to him a mere and trifling misdemeanor, the famous sorcerer Abaris had, most recently, transformed him into the likeness of a hideous Rosmarin.

Where, then, to travel? What snug and safe haven might the wide world afford for one such as Gaglioffo?

Well, they knew nothing concerning his chequered past and dubious scruples in the Kingdom of the Franks . . . and two sacks filled with fat, lustrous rubies (however acquired) would doubtless earn for him the hospitality and the favor of princes.

He resolved to venture thither, and so commanded the wyverns.

The iron chariot whirled once above the rooftops of the town, then dwindled rapidly into the west.

I will not bother to bore my readers with a description of the long and tedious descent of the mountains performed by Sir Kesrick, Princess Arimaspia, and Felixmarte of Hyrcania. Suffice it to say that they dangled from precipices, slid down beds of loose gravel, clambered painfully from crag to crag, wormed their way through crevices, and, in time, eventually reached the wooded hills at the foot of the Alps, where a dark and gloomy forest stood.

They were completely exhausted, and quite famished by now, the three of them; but they had escaped from the Giant's cook-pot, and that was the only thing that mattered. They found a foaming pool, fed from above by the

A Hospitable Friar

cataract that served the giant as his well, and washed the dirt and dust of travel from themselves, and drank deeply, and rested.

"Now, if we only had something to eat, I should be quite happy," groaned Felixmarte, rubbing his empty stomach.

"I could not agree with you more, sir knight," Arimaspia said wistfully. "It has been such a long time since I last tasted meat that I am convinced my tongue has forgotten the savor."

The three looked about at the silent boughs of the dark, wild forest. The small, careless birds, or fat rabbits, or squirrels, or whatever, that they might conceivably have brought down with a pebble or two in an improvised sling (for none of them were armed with bow and arrow) were all alseep in their nests or burrows by this hour, and it was too dark to find fruits or nuts or berries, save by random chance.

Therefore, resolving to sleep on empty stomachs as best they could, the three entered the woods and began to search for a secure and comfortable place to spend what remained of the night.

Instead they saw the light of a fire flickering between the boles of tall trees. Unlimbering his enchanted sword and taking the lead, Sir Kesrick moved as silently as he could through the underbrush, with his companions not far behind him. What might be found about the fire he could not guess—robbers, bandits, outlaws, werewolves—there was no telling.

But, if there was no food to share, the fire would at least afford them warmth and light and security of a sort.

A Hospitable Friar

What they found was a surprise, and a considerable relief. No bandits or robbers, but a small man of medium weight and middle age, roasting a plump partridge over a small fire. He wore a friar's habit and his hair was trimmed in a neat tonsure. Some little distance away, a fat mule browsed, munching the lush grass and turning upon the newcomers a placid, incurious gaze.

Having noticed their approach, he rose to his feet and did them courtesy, modestly averting his eyes from the tempting nudity of the Scythian Princess.

"Be welcome at my fire, an ye come in peace; and if ye come not in peace, then get ye gone," said the friar.

They gravely saluted him with a courtesy equal to his own, and declared themselves well-meaning travelers and strangers to these parts, but newly escaped from a giant's cook-pot. He bade them seat themselves about the small, cheerful fire and gave his name as Friar Althotas.

"Having so fortunately escaped from being a Giant's dinner, perchance you would care to partake of my own," he invited graciously, and began plucking and eviscerating the second partridge, which he rubbed with thyme and basil drawn from a smallish pouch which hung at his girdle.

"A poor meal, I suppose, but better than nothing at all," he murmured. Sir Felixmarte cleared his throat and, in deference to the Friar's churchly office, quoted an appropriate passage from Scripture:

"Not at all, sir friar! 'The moon has spots on

A Hospitable Friar

it, but remains a credible luminary.' " Then he added deferentially, "St. Cornelius Agrippa, 14:21." The Friar smiled with genuine pleasure.

"Well put, sir knight! And how interesting to encounter a youth of such scholarly and theological learning. I see that you prefer the New Testament, whereas I tend to favor the Old. But, then, and after all, as the Prophet Trismegistus remarks (2nd. Tris., 11:91) 'How absurd that wise men should quarrel about facts and hold different opinions on the same things.' "

Felixmarte flushed and looked a bit shame-faced.

"*Touché,*" chuckled Kesrick to the Hyrcanian knight, who should have known better than to attempt to match Scriptural quotations with a man of the cloth.

Then Sir Felixmarte laughed self-deprecating-ly: it was the first time that they had ever known the melancholy young knight to so much as smile, much less to laugh at his own discomfiture.

12

Conversation in a Wood

Their host the Friar noticed their amused expression, and, as if he had somehow divined the current of their thoughts, he spoke up.

"My young friend, as the Prophet Zoroaster so wisely puts it, 'A man who can laugh, if only at himself, is never really miserable.' 1st. Zoro., 107:4. And now let us *eat*."

"Yes indeed, sir friar," urged Arimaspia, who was famished from the exertions and perils of the long, long day. "Before the wolves, or Something even worse, come to chase us away from our meal."

Sir Felixmarte glanced around the gloom-drenched woods a bit dubiously. In sooth, they were uncommonly silent, for woods. But the warmth of the fire, the delectable mouth-watering aroma of roasting fowl, and the good companionship they shared, all combined to impel him to assay another quotation.

" 'It is never too late. Do it even now, and if

Conversation in a Wood

you do not live to enjoy it, somebody else will.'
St. Albertus Magnus, 1st. Epistle, 3:19.''

"What a cheerful thought," muttered Arimaspia around a delicious mouthful of well-cooked
beast. The Friar nodded, chewing; he uncorked
a bottle of decent vintage and they passed it
around the fire.

"The woods are indeed quiet tonight, but I
trust it is only due to the fact that there are
giants about. Still, Sir Felixmarte, to match your
verse, I might cite the Prophet Apollonius
Tyanaeus (4:32), to the effect that: 'The absence
of noise is not in all cases the same as
the presence of peace.' ''

About at that point, they became too busy
with eating to spare breath for further conversation.

Finishing their meal, and the last drop from
the Friar's bottle, they sat drowsily around the
fire ruminating and digesting. The Friar suggested they relate something of their travels
and adventures.

"As for myself," he explained, "I have been
looking after the parish of one of my brethren
down south, and now, on my journey home, I
have decided to go a bit farther, to the capital
of the famous Kingdom of Paflagonia, in order
to visit my old mentor, the Archbishop of
Blombodinga. Not much in the way of adventures to relate, I fear. We of the clergy seldom
become embroiled with such perils and exploits as you wandering knights—and princesses, of course!"

In a few terse, well-chosen words, Sir Kesrick

told of what had heretofore befallen the Princess Arimaspia and himself during the course of their travels, then turned to Felixmarte.

"You have not, as yet, told us aught of your own adventures, or anything concerning the enchantment of your misfortunate lady-love," he remarked interestedly. "Pray tell us somewhat concerning your quest."

Felixmarte, by now considerably more cheerful than the gloomy and swordless young knight they had rescued from the giant's cook-pot, was in a more talkative frame of mind, now that it seemed they were more or less out of danger.

"Well, sir knight and m'lady, and sir friar, my tale, while woeful enough, will not be very long in the telling," he began. "The ravishing Princess Lunetta, the younger daughter of King Bardondon and Queen Balanice is, if I may say so in all modesty, not only deeply enamored of my unworthy self, but also, at sixteen, the loveliest princess in the wide-wayed world—present company excepted, of course," he added, with a polite nod in Arimaspia's direction. "When she had reached her first birthday, as is the general custom in the lands about, her royal father and mother arranged a birthday party and made very careful to dispatch engraved invitations to every fairy in the kingdom. As often happens, in such cases, they inadvertently left one out: the Fairy Concaline.

"Oh, dear," sighed Arimaspia, who had heard something of the reputation of this vindictive and wicked old fairy.

"No one had seen or heard aught of Dame

Conversation in a Wood

Concaline in sixty years or so, and it was the general consensus of opinion, even among the fairies themselves, that she had either withered away from sheer venom, or had removed to some distant part of the world. Well, as you may have anticipated, during the festivities, when the good fairies were vying the one with the other to shower gifts upon the Princess Lunetta—hair like a fleece of gold, eyes as blue as April skies, a compexion that would make the petals of the magnolia look sallow in comparison, etc., etc.—who should appear, but Dame Concaline.

"Who indeed, alas," murmured the Friar Althotas in sympathy.

"She was old and stooped over, and ugly as sin, with a huge nose covered with warts, and she was wrapped in a rusty black gown with toads and vipers stuffed in her pockets, leaning upon a crooked staff carved all over with ominous signs," continued Felixmarte.

"A deathly silence fell over the festive throng, as the wicked old uninvited fairy came hobbling up to where the baby lay, cooing and laughing and playing with her adorable pink little toes, in her crib.

" 'Lack-a-Mercy,' croaked the withered and bad-tempered old crone, 'and it do be seemin' that all the fine ladies here has given they blessin' but pore old Concaline. So I'll be bein' brief about it, so as not to be a-holdin' up the festivities much longer.'

"And then," continued Felixmarte, after a brief, glum silence, she said something-or-other to the effect that Lunetta should be even as her namesake, the Moon, to wax and wane with the phases—or whatever the astrologers call 'em.''

Another glum silence.

"And?" prompted the friar, absorbed in the tale which was, after all, in the fine old tradition.

Felixmarte shrugged helplessly, and spread his hands.

"When the moon is full, my beloved Lunetta is of perfectly normal weight for a maiden of her size and age. But as the moon begins to wane toward a crescent, she becomes lighter and lighter, until at last they have to tie her by one ankle to the topmost turret of the Royal Palace, lest she drift away on the breeze . . ."

Kesrick looked thoughtful.

"Poor girl," sighed Arimaspia.

"What a pity!" murmured the friar, sympathetically.

"Quite," said Felixmarte. "So . . . I have been roaming the world for thirty kingdoms 'round, in search of some cure to alleviate her unfortunate condition; alas, without locating any spell or charm or remedy that will suffice. In a word, my friends, the wicked fairy has defeated Felixmarte of Hyrcania!"

The friar tut-tutted gently. And he ventured upon one more verse from Scripture which seemed to offer hope.

" 'Only he who has known defeat can achieve victory,' " he murmured. "I quote from the New Testament, which you seem fonder of than the Old."

"I know," sighed the melancholy knight. "St. Paracelsus, 17:4."

By this time they were all quite sleepy, and

Conversation in a Wood

decided to rest until daybreak. The Friar drew extra blankets from the saddle-bags heaped near his mule, and they wrapped themselves in these and curled up around the fire, which still burned merrily, shedding its cheerful orange light to struggle against the darkness.

They awoke with dawn to the chirping of birds and the rustle of dry leaves, where small squirrels or whatever scampered busily about in the underbrush, pursuing their little errands.

They all felt rested and refreshed. During the pre-dawn hours, true, they had been briefly aroused as the earth shook to the slow, uncertain rhythm of a ponderous tread as something huge went by in the dark. It was probably the Giant Stumbleduffer on his way home from the house of Thunderthighs, listing ever so slightly to port from the scores of hogsheads of strong ale he had imbibed at the table of his generous host.

Once he seemed to trip over a minor Alp and, from the deep bass rumble of his curses, they surmised that he had stubbed his toe against that obstacle in the dark. As he was nowhere in their immediate vicinity, they lay drowsily listening as his slow, stumbling steps receded in the direction of his own home in the Zetzelststein Mountains.

Thon thoy rolled over and went back to sleep.

With dawn, everything looked brighter, of course, for it was. They found ripe fruits in the woods nearby, and Friar Althotas located a fine wedge of cheese in the bottom of his saddle-bags that he had forgotten was there, and this meal, washed down with fresh cold water from a nearby spring, sufficed to restore them all to good spirits.

Here their roads must part, for the friar was going in one direction while they were bound in the other, that is, due west, toward Bohemia first of all, and then on to Dragonrouge in the country of the Franks. They bade the friar farewell as he saddled up his plump mule and prepared to depart. He gave Felixmarte a kindly pat on the shoulder.

"Would that I could somehow be of assistance to you and to your weightless princess," he sighed, "but, alas, removing curses and erasing enchantments is not at all in my line of work, I fear."

"Oh, that's all right," sighed the young Hyrcanian.

"One morsel of Scripture popped into my head during my dreams last night," he added helpfully. "For the life of me, I cannot see how it applies to your predicament, and to that of the Princess of Bohemia, but I offer it to you. Perchance wits younger than mine can see something in it that eludes me."

"What is it, pray tell?" inquired Arimaspia.

"A bit of something from St. Merlin," said the Friar. "To wit: 'Two ills can sometimes make a cure.' "

" *'Two ills can sometimes make a cure,'* " repeated the Scythian Princess. "By Mother Apia, I can see nothing in it that applies to poor Lunetta's condition, or to Sir Felixmarte's quest!"

"Neither, I must confess, do I," said the Friar

Conversation in a Wood

unhappily. "But keep it in mind, anyway. At some point, it may come in handy. And now, farewell!"

He vanished amid the trees, waving good-bye and thumping his heels in the fat flanks of his humble little steed.

They turned their faces west, and began to walk. It would be quite a long walk, to be sure, since most of Europe lay between them and their destination, but lacking steeds, there was naught to do but take Shank's mare.

13

Of Friends and Foes

Although Sir Mandricardo and Callipygia, mounted on Bayardetto, rode as swiftly as they might
across the fields and through the forests, following close upon the unmistakable tracks of the
Giant Thunderthighs who had so cavalierly carried off their companions to sweeten his cook-
pot, they were outdistanced in no time by the
famous Wizard of the Pyrénées, mounted between the strong and tireless wings of the
Hippogriff.

Atlantes soon reached the castle of the giant,
for it could have been no other, due to its
immensity; circling the enormous structure, he
searched within by use of his magical powers,
but found no sign of the evanished knight and
his lady-love. If they had ever been there, they
were either by now devoured or had somehow
managed to effect their escape from durance
vile.

Of Friends and Foes

He flew back to find the Tartar knight and the Amazon girl.

The skies had paled from dimmest mauve to dusty gold and night was falling, before Mandricardo and Callipygia yielded to weariness and decided to give over their search in order to obtain much needed rest and refreshment for themselves and for their steed, which, not being a magical hybrid of fabulous breed, was not as tireless as was Brigadore.

They made their camp by a small copse of beech-trees, and the arrows of Callipygia soon brought down a brace of mallards, which they plucked, eviscerated, washed clean in a small mountain freshet, and were broiling over a small fire when the Hippogriff landed near their small encampment and old Atlantes climbed stiffly from the saddle, to confess his failure to locate our missing hero and heroine.

They made the best meal of it that they could, under these grim circumstances; indeed, Atlantes summoned by sorcery to their side two bottles of the finest vintage the cellars of his Iron Castle contained. They ate and drank heartily, conversing little, as the sunset flames died and the first, few, faint stars were lit and hung in their appointed places.

"Well, dash it all," grumbled the Tartar, "by now, surely, the giant has cooked and eaten them, since you say they were nowhere in the monster's castle, what?"

"I think not," replied Atlantes. "My magical senses have been honed to a nicety: there was no taste of *meat* in the giant's cook-pot. Seemed to be a vegetable stew, in fact."

"Then, sir wizard, it is your considered opinion that the gallant Sir Kesrick and his beauteous princess somehow escaped the clutches of Thunderthighs?" inquired Callipygia.

"Indeed, madame," said the magician. "But 'tis too dark to hope to trace their progress from the air. There is a deep, dark wood which stands at the foot of the mountain, but we shall have to wait until dawn lights the world, to pursue them farther."

He did not say whether he thought the quest was hopeless, but something in his tones cast Sir Mandricardo into the depths of despair.

"I say, dash it all, a bad business, what?" exclaimed the noble-hearted Tartar. Callipygia gave him a searching glance from under level brows.

"Surely, the Code of Chivalry requires that we continue the search until the very last chance of rescue has been exhausted," she murmured. Mandricardo straightened as if stung by a hornet.

"By my halidom," he swore feelingly, "but I would not give up the search for our lost friends—not for all the rubies in the crown of Prester John!"

They believed him sincere, and gave up the matter until dawn.

As it happened, they did not have to camp out in the field, rolled into blankets around the bonfire, as had their friends, Kesrick and Princess Arimaspia. For Atlantes, whose old bones ached after an unaccustomed day in the Hippogriff's saddle, conjured up silken pavilions for them to spend the night in.

Of Friends and Foes

He uttered sonorous words in a tongue unknown to them, and made mystic gestures. Suddenly, there appeared amidst the meadows three capacious pavilions, one of red and black silk, in the colors of Tartary, one in gray and silver, for Atlantes himself, and one in green and gold, which were the national colors of Amazonia.

Entering their respective pavilions, Mandricardo and his lady discovered luxurious carpets, side tables laden with silver bowls of fresh fruit, and soft couches strewn with many plump cushions.

They also discovered bathtubs of copper filled with hot, soapy water, wherein for a time they luxuriated, washing away the sweat and stains of travel. Whereafter, they slept soundly, waking at dawn to find that the magic of Atlantes had provided them with superb breakfasts.

Callipygia awoke to the indescribably delicious odors of hot chocolate simmering in silver urns, and hot buttered toast, with strawberries in whipped cream, and sliced, smoking ham. She made a sumptuous meal of it all.

As for Mandricardo, he awoke to fried eggs, rashers of succulent bacon done to a crisp, a pot of fragrant tea, and buttermilk biscuits dipped in dripping honey.

Atlantes himself made his morning repast from lightly scrambled eggs, toasted corn muffins, tiny sausages, a bowl of sliced oranges from the Hesperides buried in frosty snow plucked moments before from the crests of Mount Caucasus. His drink, by the way, was a fat pot of fresh, steaming hot coffee, despite the fact that this beverage was as yet unknown in the world's west. A wizard, Atlantes was a close personal friend of the Grand Inca, and was most welcome in Manoa and in El Dorado, to say nothing of Norumbega and the Seven Cities of Cibola, and thus was well acquainted with the pleasures of hot coffee in the mornings.

They finished their separate meals with a sigh of pleasant repletion, and I dare give as my opinion that both Sir Mandricardo and the Amazon girl, Callipygia, may have bethought to themselves that knightly and heroic adventurings were one thing, but that if you must be embarked on one, it is certainly nice to have a powerful and potent magician along to take care of certain of the creature comforts.

That most pitiful and friendless of all Paynims, Gaglioffo, in the meanwhile, was faring much less comfortably than were Mandricardo and his companions.

Since escaping from the village gaol in the magical flying wyvern-drawn chariot, Gaglioffo had given his steeds their head and let them fly where they would, since one part of the (to him) unknown west of the world was no better and no worse than any other. At length, wearying of flight, the dragonish creatures had brought to earth the iron chariot, and, devouring a few toads, serpents and scorpions, had tucked their heads under their batlike wings, and gone to a well-deserved sleep, leaving the hapless—and by now quite hungry—Paynim to his own devices.

He found himself, under skies of peach and

Of Friends and Foes

tangerine flame, amid a barren plain unwatered by any streams, where few trees flourished, and none of them, as he discovered, the sort that bear fruit or berries or edible nuts.

He slept, therefore, under the chariot itself, with the bare hard ground for mattress, whimpering and complaining of his sore and numerous grievances to Mahoum, and Termagant, and others of his pagan Idols.

And awoke a little after dawn, his paunch a-grumble with pangs of hunger, his throat parched, and stiff and sore in every bone and joint.

Such also, it would seem, are the rewards of dastardy!

As for Sir Kesrick's fairy godmother, the Dame Pirouetta, she was having a difficult time of it too, for all her fairy powers. Her glittering magical Cloud had unfolded into being first upon the rolling plains of Bohemia, at the spot where Sir Kesrick and the Scythian Princess had been snatched from their saddle by the giant; finding nothing, she had thence directed the Cloud to locate the godson for whom she was searching, whereupon it transported her to the castle of Thunderthighs, where he slept late, snoring like distant thunderstorms over many an empty hogshead of strong ale.

Then the Cloud had carried her to an empty glade in the forest below the Alps where there remained nothing but the ashes of a burnt-out fire and a few feathers, left over from the meal which Kesrick and Arimaspia and their friend, the young knight of Hyrcania, had shared the night before. But no sign of the godson whose whereabouts she anxiously sought.

"Drat!" said the good fairy to herself in vexation. "The mischievous lad is moving about more quickly than even my Magic Cloud can follow him. Whenever I catch up with the young rapscallion, I shall have a word or two to say to him—!"

14

Castle of Enchantment

The two knights and the Scythian Princess
passed through the woods and wound their
way through heavily wooded hills, into a re-
gion of broad, grassy plains, watered by many
small streams and freshets. None of them were
accustomed to going afoot, and erelong all three
were weary of this mode of travel.

Particularly Sir Kesrick, who had the burden
of his long mailcoat of Gnomish work. For once,
he felt fortunate that he had lost his lance and
that his shield was still (insofar as he knew)
slung over the saddlehorn of Brigadore.

As for Sir Felixmarte, the Hyrcanian had
been snatched up by the Giant Thunderthighs
while sleeping under a tree, and he had set
aside sword, shield, helm and much of his
armor; he was, therefore, less burdened than
was the Frankish knight.

Arimaspia, of course, wore nothing, and of

the three it was the princess who found the going easiest.

They did not know exactly where they were, for one hill looks very much like another, and the same is true of fields and streams, but from the inclination of the sun they were aware that they were traveling, albeit more slowly than they could have wished, in the right direction.

Along the way so far they had encountered no cottages or hovels and there were no plowed fields or farms in view. But then, on the other hand, they had as yet encountered no dangerous predators, either, and so they felt reasonably lucky.

Along toward noontime, they found themselves entering another wood, and this time it was a deep and dark one, and thickly grown. The intertangled boughs overhead, laden with heavy foliage, cut out the light of day and the bushes between the boles of the tall and very ancient trees made the going difficult, especially for Arimaspia.

"Now, what in the world—!" marveled Sir Kesrick, stopping short. He stared, and they with him.

Quite suddenly, the forest had divulged a trimmed and clipped hedge of thornbushes, twice taller than a man. This could only be the sign of human habitation, and the hospitality of whoever might dwell here could, perhaps, be anticipated.

For a time, they followed the hedge, eventually discovering a gate of what they could have sworn was *solid silver*. There was no slug-horn nor bell for them to sound, but Arimaspia, whose

Castle of Enchantment

feet were sore and who wished mightily to sit down and have a cold drink, pushed against the bars, and the gate opened to her touch as if by magic.

Peering within, they saw meadows which stretched off to a considerable distance on every side, and a road of clean and freshly raked gravel which stretched before them into the hazy distance and seemed to beckon invitingly.

Nothing ventured, nothing gained, is (or ought to be) the motto of knightly adventurers. Therefore they entered and began to follow the gravel road, all of them, that is, save for Arimaspia, who, bare foot, much preferred to tread upon the lush, dewy grasses beside the gravel path.

Erelong they came to an enormous and very ancient castle of hoary stone, overgrown with what looked like centuries of ivy. As they approached, fountains began to spout and splash in stone basins which had heretofore been dry. The portal was an immense slab of waxed centuries-old oak, which opened noiselessly at a touch.

"We seem welcome enough," mused Kesrick. He called out a greeting, to which there returned no answer but many solemn echoes. They ventured within, finding themselves at one end of a high-roofed hall, whose stone walls were lined with age-blackened oil portraits interspersed with suits of armor. Candelabra protruded from the walls on bronze fixtures, and as they ventured down the hall, these were lit one by one, and by invisible hands.

"This must be the palace of some powerful sorcerer," whispered Felixmarte. Kesrick nodded.

"But not, apparently, an unfriendly one," he observed.

At the end of the long hall they found themselves in a wide circular room like a rotunda. A fireplace of carven gray marble was set into one wall, with a fire snapping cheerily upon the grate, although there seemed to be no one about. Before the fire, a table was drawn, set with snowy damask. Crystal goblets and decanters, superb silver, and porcelain plates and dishes were already laid out for three. There were also three tall chairs of carved oak with seats and backs of padded brocade drawn up to the table.

At their tentative approach, all three chairs moved out a little as if in silent but eloquent invitation.

"Goodness," breathed Arimaspia. "We certainly do seem to be welcome enough, but where is our host?"

Neither of her companions could answer that question, but the delectable odors of hot soup came from the tureens and the aroma of cooked meats and sauces and gravies from the many covered dishes.

They seated themselves, staring around them in bewilderment. The walls of the rotunda were hung with worn and faded tapestries. Fresh dry rushes were strewn upon the stone-paved floor, and aromatic herbs had been sprinkled upon them. The savory odors of the foods—which seemed to have been taken from the ovens only moments before—assaulted their nostrils.

Excellent wines stood in crystal decanters,

Castle of Enchantment

buried to their necks in silver buckets filled with crushed ice.

Kesrick shrugged, and helped himself. "Champagne?" he asked, and poured three goblets full. Arimaspia served the soup, which was of cream and asparagus and spiced with chives and thyme, and unutterably delicious. Felixmarte curiously removed the lid from a huge platter and found a roast suckling pig with a baked apple in its mouth, done to perfection. With a happy sigh, he picked up a silver knife and began to carve.

There followed a fish course in lemon butter, seasoned flawlessly, and vegetables in cream gravy, and a crisp and frosty salad with oil and vinegar, and some sort of small fowl on skewers, and they drank champagne with the pork, white wine with the fish, and red wine with the fowl, regardless of official propriety.

From time to time they glanced about, expecting their unseen host to make his appearance at any moment, but he remained absent. As none of the three adventurers had enjoyed so sumptuous a meal in many, many days, they ate with a hearty appetite and thoroughly enjoyed the feast.

After the meal, there were ripe fruit in silver bowls and hot, flaky pastries steaming and stuffed with cinnamon-spiced slices of apples, and nine kinds of sherbet poured over shaved ice. Then followed hot, fragrant coffee, which they found novel and interesting.

All the while, the fire blazed on the grate. From time to time, a log would collapse into white ash, and every time this happened invisible hands replaced it with a fresh log.

After their lunch—if one can insult so splendid a repast by calling it merely "lunch"—three doors which they had not previously noticed opened in the rotunda walls. Peering into one, Arimaspia found a dainty boudoir and a porcelain tub in which a bath had just been drawn. It was filled with hot, soapy water and she sighed blissfully as she submerged herself therein. Unseen hands scrubbed her back with a sponge while yet other invisible servitors shampooed and dried and combed and brushed her golden hair.

Kesrick and Felixmarte investigated the other two rooms and found more manly accommodations, as well as steaming, sudsy baths obviously drawn for them. Without further ado, the two knights shucked off their mail and other garments, and wallowed in the rare luxury of a hot bath.

When they arose therefrom, viewless hands enfolded them in soft, heated towels. They discovered that fresh garments had been laid out for them, Kesrick's including a fine new surcoat of claret-red satin trimmed with gray fur, Felixmarte's of brown velvet the color of cloves. After such a long time on the road, it was unutterably pleasant for both knights to don fresh garments and undergarments.

They also noticed that, while they had been enjoying their baths, their mail or armor had been scrubbed and oiled and, here and there, the ravages of battle and adventure had been skillfully repaired.

Castle of Enchantment

Their gratitude to their unknown benefactor knew, as the saying has it, no bounds.

Emerging from their rooms, they discovered the Princess Arimaspia preening in front of a long mirror that had not previously made its existence known. She was wearing a long gown of sapphire-blue taffeta the precise shade of her lovely eyes, with a low-cut bodice trimmed with ivory-hued lace. She looked exquisite, and she knew it

Since Sir Kesrick had heretofore only seen his lady-love completely nude, he found the sight of her modestly clothed oddly tantalizing and also titillating.

Through the tall casements of the hall it could be seen that the shadows of afternoon were gradually lengthening across velvety lawns where white peacocks strolled languidly. Evening was nigh.

"We could stay the night, I suppose," said Arimaspia dreamily.

"We could; but I think it best that we be on our way. We have, after all, many more leagues to go," replied Kesrick.

"Oh, dear—by Petosyrus, but I suppose you're right!" she sighed. It was so easy, after such a long time of doing without them, to become accustomed to the luxuries and comforts of civilized life.

On their way out, the travelers found themselves in vast gardens where ten thousand roses bloomed, each more splendid and more perfect than the last. They were of every shade from snowy white to mellow ivory, yellow, gold, pink, rich crimson. Arimaspia had never seen such superb blooms and wanted to pick one and take it with her, if only as a souvenir of this happy afternoon.

It is perhaps very fortunate that she thought better of it and left their host's glorious roses untouched. . . .

15

Mandricardo's Monster

The Tartar knight and the Amazon girl awoke the next morning to discover that the magician Atlantes had already arisen. While the famous Wizard of the Pyrénées was not accustomed to arising at so early an hour, his old bones and joints were aching him, and it was entirely due to the pangs of rheumatism that he had wakened at dawn.

Magicians such as Atlantes, it seems, can prolong their term of earthly existence far beyond the normal span allotted to ordinary men. But joints are joints, nonetheless, and age will take its toll in one way, if not in another.

The two lovers rose from their slumbers to discover that Atlantes had already commanded service from the invisible spirits that attended him. That is, a table was set—having melted out of nowhere, for it had certainly not been there the night before—and was laden with crisp linen, sparkling silver, and dishes of gold.

There was hot chocolate in a golden teapot, and hot buttered toast, and rashers of crisp, succulent bacon, and scrambled eggs, and nine kinds of jam, jellies and preserves, and—I don't know what else. They broke their fast with gusto and dined sumptuously, nearly as well as had Kesrick and Arimaspia and Sir Felixmarte at their luncheon in the enchanted castle.

When they were done, and the last drop was drunk and the last scrap of food devoured, Mandricardo sat back with a hearty sigh of repletion, and, surreptitiously, let out the two top buttons of what he wore in lieu of trousers, which had not yet become popular, anyway. He felt at peace with the whole world; but Callipygia was more than a trifle curious.

Watching the empty plates and the crumpled napkins, and, indeed, the very table itself, whisk themselves out of existence, it occurred to the Amazon girl to inquire why, since Atlantes could perform such miraculous feats as summoning entire meals-for-three out of empty air, he had not done so the other night—when, as you may recall, it had been her own prowess with bow and arrow that had brought down the fowl which had served them for supper.

Atlantes chuckled.

"Perhaps, madame, my existence has been a rather sheltered one in recent generations!" he observed dryly. "When you can command splendid meals out of nothingness, you become, may I say, satiated on delicacies. And, since I have embarked upon this adventure, it seemed to me interesting to enjoy a rude but hearty meal,

Mandricardo's Monster

cooked in the open air. And enjoy it I did, and with relish!

"Also," he added slyly, "from the way that Mistress Callipygia eagerly unlimbered her bow of yestereve, and stalked off into the wilderness to procure game for our meal, methinks she wished to demonstrate her skills in bringing home (as the saying goes) the, ah, bacon."

The Amazon girl flushed, then grinned, displaying adorable dimples. This was exactly true, and it had pleased her pride enormously to have been able to prove her prowess with the bow the night before. Still and all, licking the last crumb of perfect toast from the corner of her mouth, and thinking nostalgically of the gorgeous hot chocolate, she rather wished that she had let the Wizard of the Pyrénées provide their nutriment. . . .

Atlantes, his stomach filled and his rheumatics at their rest, was eager to be up and aloft on the traces of the missing Frankish knight and his lady-love. Mandricardo assisted the old magician to don his gleaming armor and helped him into the saddle of Brigadore, who, for his part, having feasted no less splendidly than they on the fresh, dewy grasses, was anxious to be aloft and away in search of his master and mistress.

The two dwindled into the clear, sparkling air of morning, and Mandricardo and Callipygia were not far behind in climbing into Bayardetto's saddle and setting off. They cantered across the plain, and the Tartar knight sighed blissfully:

"Oh, I say, old girl, how jolly good life is! To

have a knightly quest, what? To prick manfully across the trackless plain in search of adventures, for maidens to rescue and lost comrades-in-arms to assist out of, you know, dangers and perils!" he exclaimed zestfully.

Callipygia turned in the saddle to give him a look.

"So long as the maiden you rescue is the lady-love of Sir Kesrick and not some other hussy, all is well," she observed rather frostily.

"Oh, I say, old girl, what!" he chirped cheerfully. They rode off across the plain in the general direction of the east, still following the Giant's footprints.

And came upon a Monster!

It was a Unicorn; and not one of your dainty, pretty, little silken-white Unicorns, either. They are fit only for postcards or pictures in children's books: this was your real, true Unicorn, as first described by wise Ctesias centuries before: dangerous as a bear, big as a house, and with a horn long enough, sharp enough and strong enough to impale an elephant, if need be .

It was, in point of fact, the very near relative of the common or garden Unicorn, properly known to the students of unnatural history as the Monoceros. While still vaguely horselike in its appearance, its hide was not sleek and silky, but leathery and tough. And it was huge and heavy and strong.

Also, it was in a bad temper.

"Good-oh!" exclaimed Sir Mandricardo. "How jolly, what? Let me drop you here, m'love, whilst I give challenge to this dreadsome creature, eh?"

Mandricardo's Monster

Callipygia, who could handle her short-bladed Amazonian sword as ably as could any man, bit her tongue and kept silent, although it was a struggle. She had fallen madly in love with the Tartar knight, Amazon or no Amazon, and was beginning to understand that men have their pride in prowess even as do Amazons.

So she slid meekly from the saddle and stood, gazing with admiration, real or feigned, as her stalwart champion snapped down the vizor of his helm, donned shield and snatched up spear, sank his rowels into the sleek sides of Bayardetto, and cantered off across the plain to, if not do battle against the Monoceros, at least to bellow his chivalric challenge.

The fact that the monster was bigger than a brace of bulls did not deter his enthusiasm for the contest.

Now the Monoceros, as has just been remarked upon, was in a rather foul temper that morning. An hour or two earlier, it had been hunting for hippopotami along the upper headwaters of the River Indus down in Hindoostan, and had found no luck. Monoceroses enjoy a succulent and tasty snack of hippopotamus-flank from time to time, it seems, and the frustration of not being quite able to capture one of the juicy creatures still rankled in the breast of Mandricardo's monster.

Hence, when the Monoceros, piggy little eyes for once alert, spotted the knight in gleaming armor cantering across the plain toward its mudhole, wherein it was at present wallowing, its sullen temper flared into monocerontic rage.

It came out of the mud, neighing like a

steamwhistle, and headed toward the mortal annoyance, fat, short legs waddling with amazing speed, and, by the way, shaking the earth, ever so slightly, beneath its weight.

Now, Bayardetto was a veteran warhorse, and knew how to handle himself in battle, mélee, siege, foray, or whatever. Had his master been spurring him into conflict with another mounted knight, the strong, intelligent black stallion would have held steady to the course and gone about his horsely duty.

But a Monoceros charging directly at one has an unsettling effect on any horse, even one so staunch and disciplined as Bayardetto. Who, quite naturally, swerved to one side to permit the thundering hooves of the immense monster to rush by.

"Oh, I say, dash it all!" cried Sir Mandricardo in vexation. He reined his steed in and turned his head about and spurred him into the fray once again.

Snorting like a water buffalo in heat, the Monoceros turned about, swerving ponderously, and charged at knight and rider once again. And once again the intelligent warhorse, and quite sensibly, avoiding the encounter with something that could easily have gone over him and his rider as a steam engine goes over an automobile.

"By my halidom, horse, what ails you?" cried Mandricardo fretfully. And, once again, he headed his trusty steed toward the lumbering monster which had, once again, managed to halt its clumsy stride and turn about, to charge them.

Mandricardo's Monster

By this time, it must be admitted, Mandricardo was sweating in his armor, and the leveled spear was becoming heavier and heavier in his grip. Nonetheless, blinking the perspiration from his eyes fiercely, kneeing Bayardetto forcibly, he hurtled once again toward his monstrous and ill-tempered adversary—

—Who unaccountably swerved a little to one side!

And headed toward where Callipygia stood, knee-deep in the thick grass, hands clasped, in admiration for her hero's bravery, between her two magnificent breasts.

The Amazon girl had not even drawn her own sword; and now there was not time enough to do so.

For, with the irresistible weight and velocity of an avalanche thundering down the flanks of one or another Alp, the Monoceros came surging down upon Callipygia, moving with a rapidity that seemed uncanny for a brute of such tonnage.

BOOK FOUR

THE LIGHTER-THAN-AIR PRINCESS

16

Befriending a Dragon

Along toward mid-morning, Kesrick and his companions were footsore and heartily weary of traveling by Shank's mare. Never had the two knights or the princess more earnestly appreciated the comfort and convenience of riding hither and thither and yon on horseback. Or, in Sir Kesrick's case, Hippogriff-back. But there was nothing that they could do about it, but limp on, sweating in their mail.

This part of the countryside became bleak and barren; the earth folded itself into rocky ridges cleft asunder by steep ravines. The air was dry and sultry with curious vagrant whiffs of sulfur and brimstone on every other breeze.

For a time they were able to traverse the ravines by jumping across them, for they were narrow. At length, however, they came to one that was wider—so wide that it would take wings to get to the other side.

"What now?" sighed Arimaspia. And just then

another whiff of brimstone—stronger and more pungent than any before—curled up from the pit before them. They peered curiously over the edge and were frozen to the marrow by a horrendous and unexpected sight.

At the very bottom of the ravine, a dragon lay sprawled and apparently napping. It was nowhere near the size of Dzoraug, the Great-Grandfather of All Dragons, with whom Kesrick had conversed on an earlier adventure at the easternmost Edge of the World. But it was certainly big enough, measuring some thirty-eight paces from wrinkled snout to barbed tail tip.

"Oh, my," said the Scythian Princess in faint tones.

The creature was covered with scales the size of dinner plates, and was dark red all over, fading to grayish-yellow at the belly. Its saurian head was crowned with spikes, and a spiky ridge ran down its spine. Yellow smoke trickled from its nostrils as it snoozed: this was the source of the sulfurous-and-brimstony odor they had noticed.

It opened a sleepy eye of green fire and looked up at them. However, it made no move. And then it was that they discovered the dragon was tethered to an immense boulder by a massive chain of heavy iron, much as a watchdog might be chained before a door to guard the entrance to a residence.

At this discovery, the two knights and the Princess relaxed somewhat, and examined the monster with lively curiosity. Dragons were far more rare in their day than they once had been, and of the three of them, only Kesrick had ever

Befriending a Dragon

seen one close-to. Sir Felixmarte, who was of studious habits, as has heretofore been said, stared at the chained beast with intense scientific interest. He was well read in natural history, and knew all about dragons, from *books,* at least.

"Pray observe, Sir Kesrick," he said in interested tones. "From the smoke-blackened rocks before the brute (to say nothing of the smoke which rises from its nostrils), the monster belongs to the species *draco ignispirans,* as described by Meinheer Lycosthenes in his celebrated monograph. Signore Aldrovandus, who devotes no fewer than fifty-nine folio pages to dragons—"

"Would perhaps have pointed out that it also belongs to the species *draco volans,*" remarked Kesrick, dryly, pointing to the great wings folded against the monster's back. These closely resembled the wings of bats, ribbed and membranous, except that the dragon's wings were like thin, sheeted opal, flickering with iridescent hues.

Draco ignispirans is the scientific name for the "fire-breathing" dragon, while *draco volans* is the "winged" or "flying" dragon.

Felixmarte frowned. "Of course; you are quite right. But the two forms are seldom, if ever, combined in a single specimen! Pliny remarks on the fact . . . Physiologus, on the other hand—"

Just then the dragon cleared its throat politely, emitting a jet of sizzling sparks and several clinkers, which clattered about on the stony floor of the ravine.

"Sir Knights," it said in a hoarse voice, rather

like a ton of coal rattling down a metal chute, "you see me chained and helpless. Of your chivalry, I beg you to pass by and not to bring against me your terrible bright swords, for I cannot defend myself, and it would not be honorable for you to slay a helpless creature, monster or no."

Kesrick looked thoughtful: of course, the dragon was perfectly correct. No knight worthy of his steel would bear deadly arms against a creature, however hideous, incapable of holding his own in battle.

"Tell me, how did you come to be in these dire straits?" he inquired. The dragon sighed, singeing a dozen of the scarlet scorpions that were scuttling about the floor of the ravine, and charring a rock-viper to a crisp.

"Long centuries ago, the wicked Arcalaus the Enchanter captured me and chained me here to guard one of the approaches to his magical fortress. When the gallant Amadis destroyed the villainous Enchanter, no one thought to release me from my bondage; doubtless, they did not even know that I was here," the monster explained. A tear of fiery liquid the size of a pint went trickling down his scaly cheek

"The poor thing!" cried Arimaspia, sympathetically. The two knights exchanged quizzical glances with each other; to their way of thinking, a chained Dragon is better than one that is free to romp about the countryside and ravage the landscape. But the gentler sex are more easily moved.

Nor was Sir Kesrick's heart exactly hardened against the dragon's pitiful plight. For one thing,

the dragon was red, and the Red Dragon—
dragon-rouge—was the heraldic emblem of his
ancient line. He knew all about the celebrated
Don Amadis of Gaul, of course, from the history books; and of Arcalaus the Enchanter, too.

His mischievous green eyes sparkled with
excitement: it suddenly occurred to him that
here might well be the answer to their dilemma.

"Have you a name, monster?" he inquired.
The dragon nodded proudly.

"I am hight Gartazascus Minor, the third son
of the famous Tarasque who was himself the
brother to Crysophylax Dives, son of the distinguished—" And the dragon, before they could
stop him, rattled off his lineage (and it was an
impressive one), at least as far back as the Flood.

Kesrick politely introduced his companions
to the Red Dragon, as well as himself. He also
explained their predicament; the dragon seemed
sympathetic.

"I yearn for my freedom, sir knight," the
dragon sighed. "My brood of draklings will by
now have grown nigh unto maturity, but my
dragoness may still linger in some proximity to
our mountainous home upon Caucasus. If you
will sever my chains, I will bear you on swift
wings to your destination."

"No tricks, now!" cautioned the Frankish
knight.

"No tricks," said the dragon solemnly. "I
swear it upon your sword."

Swords are the natural enemies of dragons,
for it is by employment of those weapons that
knights slay dragons, and always have, and,
one presumes, always will—at least, as long as

there remain knights and dragons in the world. Kesrick considered; Arimaspia tugged his arm

"Surely we can trust the word of so honorable a creature," she urged. "Anyway, it's better than walking all the way to Bohemia!"

Kesrick considered the chains which bound the dragon to the bottom of the crevasse. They seemed to be of nothing stronger than iron.

"With your strength, how is it that you have not shattered your chains asunder long ere this?" he inquired.

"Because Arcalaus the Enchanter laid a spell upon them, which rendered them stronger than adamant," said the dragon woefully. Adamant is the strongest substance in the world, stronger than steel by seven hundred times, and thirty times more durable than pure diamond. Kesrick looked depressed: even the enchanted steel of Dastagerd could hardly hope to bite through adamantine chains.

But then he remembered that the pommelstone of Dastagerd was a magical gem called the Pantharb, and that because of the Pantharb, Dastagerd was known in song and story as the Sword of Undoings, for it had the power to undo enchantments.

The three discussed the matter among themselves. Arimaspia, kind-hearted princess that she was, still urged that they owed it to their knightly honor to free the poor miserable monster from its chains. Felixmarte was of similar mind.

The Dragon looked hopeful. "My lady," the creature said in its gravelly voice, "for your kindness I will foreswear to devour any damo-

Befriending a Dragon

sels for the length of my life, and especially will I eschew the devouring of princesses."

Kesrick decided to take the risk, and began to climb down the rugged side of the ravine, followed by Felixmarte and the Princess of Scythia. It was not a difficult descent, such was the crumbling nature of the rocky ledges. Reaching the floor of the ravine, he touched the pommel-stone of the Sword of Undoings against the massive links of the chain which bound Gartazascus Minor.

The enchanted metal, which had gleamed blackly silver like pure adamant, now became dull gray flecked with spots of rust.

One stroke of Dastagerd served to sever the chains as if they had been links of rotten thread.

"Free!" breathed the Red Dragon with a sigh of relief which scorched the hems of their cloaks. "I beg your pardon," he added. "Now where is it that you wish me to carry you?"

Kesrick told him; the dragon looked mystified. "I can recall no such kingdom of that name from my days of freedom," he admitted, "but, then, I have been imprisoned here for centuries, and kingdoms change their names frequently, I am told. You shall have to guide me thither. Now, climb aboard, if you please."

They were all gratified that the dragon was true to his word, for seldom are monsters honorable.

They scrambled upon its back between the wings of sheeted opal, finding the Dragon's back very hot to the touch (which was understandable, since he had a furnace in his belly).

THE LIGHTER-THAN-AIR PRINCESS

Fortunately, their clothing should serve to insulate them against his body temperature.

"Hang on carefully, please," advised the Red Dragon.

Then he spread his mighty wings and drummed the air with a sound like thunder. And soared aloft—up and out of the ravine of his long imprisonment—and into the blue sky.

17

Taming the Monoceros

Mandricardo went pricking off across the plains
to engage the Monoceros in battle, shouting out
things like "Have at you, varlet!" and "View
Halloo!" and "Yoicks!"

For its part, the Monoceros flattened its piggy
little ears and charged the knight. Considering
its tonnage, it is only natural that it took the
Monoceros some little time to get up steam, so
to speak; once it was in full charge, however,
its momentum carried it *past* the Tartar knight,
who reined about with an annoyed expression,
and hurtled in pursuit.

Realizing it had missed the knight, the huge
monster put on the brakes, and wheeled about
to charge thundering down upon Sir Mandricardo once again. And once again the two
missed each other by more than a spear's length.

Monoceroses have dim, weak little eyes, and
are as nearsighted as most giants.

For a time, arms folded against her ample

bosom, Callipygia watched without speaking as Mandricardo and the Monoceros chased each other hither, thither, and also yon. She wore a disapproving expression on her stern but handsome features as she watched her hero galloping about the plain, pursuing the lumbering monster and shouting out "Yoicks!" and "Hark forward!" and "Tantivy! Tantivy!" as if he were a fox-hunter in chase.

It riled her to be told to stay behind out of harm's way, while her hero fought the monster. For one thing, the Amazons were unaccustomed to taking orders from mere men, and, anyway, Callipygia knew that she was as good a warrior as Mandricardo. But she knew that men were sensitive about their prowess and need to show off, so she held her peace and bided her time.

After a time, nearly out of breath, the Tartar knight lost track of his foe in the whirling clouds of dust their futile pursuits of each other had churned up from the hard-packed earth, and paused to reorient himself.

As he did so, he observed a remarkable sight.

Trotting with an earth-shaking tread, the Monoceros had come within eyeshot of Callipygia, where she stood with arms folded. But instead of lowering its massive head and thundering down upon her to impale her with its one sharp horn, the monster blinked, grinned sheepishly and rolled its piggy little eyes.

Then it trotted ponderously toward her, head lowered, and, docile as a lamb, lay down at her feet and rested its massive horn in her lap—for

Taming the Monoceros

Callipygia had backed away in such surprise that she tripped over a stone and sat down heavily.

Cautiously, the Amazon girl reached out a tentative hand to stroke the leathery hide of the enormous creature who knelt worshipfully on its knees before her. The little pink eyes closed blissfully at her caress.

Sir Mandricardo reined up with a snort of surprise.

"Well, I'll be dashed!" he declared. And it occurred to him what had happened here:

A Monoceros is second cousin to a unicorn, and everyone knows that unicorns are rendered helpless by the presence of a virgin.

And Callipygia was a virgin.

The knight and his lady exchanged glances over the huge head of the fawning monster, his baffled and angry, hers smug and amused.

And *this* is why Mandricardo never added a Monoceros to the list of Ogres and Firedrakes and Witches, and whatever that he had slain.

About then, Atlantes brought the Hippogriff to earth not far from the scene of this tableau, which he regarded askance.

The Monoceros peeped slyly at him from where it knelt with its heavy head in Callipygia's lap; it wagged its short, fat tail for all the world like a puppy hopeful of play. The Wizard of the Pyrénées was in no mood for coddling monsters. He flapped his bony hands irritably.

"Shoo! Shoo, now! Begone, you nasty brute," he said. With a reluctant backwards glance at the Amazon girl, the Monoceros tucked its tail between its legs and trotted off into the distance.

"Any news of Sir Kesrick and his princess, sir wizard?" asked Mandricardo, dismounting from Bayardetto's saddle. The wizard shook his head crossly.

"Not a sign," he huffed. "Vanished from the face of Terra Magica, it seems. Saw nothing at all, except for a Dragon flying past in the general direction of the capital of Bohemia. Odd, that; wrong season for dragons, you know."

Mandricardo gallantly assisted a breathless Callipygia to her feet and helped to dust her off. The Amazon girl was a little dreamy-eyed from her miraculous taming of the Monoceros, as is only natural, as such a thing hardly happens any more often in Terra Magica than it does in the Lands We Know. They discussed their missing friends with Atlantes.

"Where could those two have possibly gotten to?' marveled the Amazon girl. The two men shook their heads glumly.

"Enchanted, perhaps," suggested Atlantes.

"Eaten by monsters," said Sir Mandricardo sorrowfully.

Just then a glittering silver Cloud unfolded itself out of thin air, making them all jump with alarm.

Mounted upon the Cloud was a tiny little old woman in a hoop-skirt several generations out of fashion, and sewn all over with a satrap's ransom in seed pearls and garnets. Her wrinkled face was heavily painted with rouge, powder and other cosmetics; a heartshaped beautyspot called attention to her thin lips. Atop her

Taming the Monoceros

head a towering peruke of powdered wig rose, shaped and twined and twisted into the likeness of a full-rigged galley under sail. In one bony hand she clasped a fairy wand of sparkling silver, tipped with a five-pointed star of scintillant diamonds

All three instantly recognized her as Pirouetta the Fairy of the Fountain, the fairy godmother of Sir Kesrick of Dragonrouge.

She surveyed the three of them with disfavor: Mandricardo, looking hot and sweaty, his mail and garments gray with dust; Atlantes looking remarkably out of place in his suit of plate-armor, his plumed helmet askew on his balding head; Callipygia, still dreamy-eyed over having been adored by the Monoceros.

"A fine lot, the three of you!" exclaimed the good fairy, shaking her wand at them. "Where is that young scallawag of a godson of mine— and his trollop of a lady-love? I've enough to do back in my enchanted palace in Brociliande, to waste time looking for lost knights and strayed princesses!"

"Damn Pirouetta," said Atlantes a bit meekly—for a fairy in a fury is something to be pacified, I assure you—"we have, ah, just been searching for the twain ourselves, without, I fear, any noteworthy result."

"I say, you know," Sir Mandricardo interjected helpfully, "they were carried off by a giant, what?"

"I know all about that," snapped Dame Pirouetta. "And they escaped, for I could find no trace of them in the giant's castle; no trace at all."

"I wonder if she looked in the giant's stomach?" whispered Callipygia to her knight, but the sharp ears of Kesrick's fairy godmother heard her remark.

"For your information, madame, that was the first place I looked," said Pirouetta acidly. "Nothing there but rather a large quantity of vegetable stew. Not to mention more hogsheads of ale than should be proper for even a giant to guzzle."

"Alas," said the Wizard of the Pyrénées, spreading his hands, "I have none of my magical implements with me, having traveled rather light, and cannot find the whereabouts of the missing two by sorcerous means."

"Hrrmph!" snorted Pirouetta. "Well-a-day, we shall have to combine forces, I see. But first, it's time for lunch!"

Gaglioffo clung whimpering and crying out to Mahoum, Golfarin and Termagant, his pudgy black fingers locked in a deathlike grip on the railing of the iron chariot. The whistling wind had whipped his turban askew and had filled his eyes with tears so that he was all but blinded.

In their joy at being free and aloft again, the matched team of Wyverns had flown first to Ultime Thule amid the Frozen Sea, then due south to the Antipodes, and were now doubling back and were (Gaglioffo thought) somewhere over the regions which paid homage to the Emperor Contalabutte. They were nigh upon the borders of the famous Kingdom of the Franks before he summoned up enough presence of mind to sound the little silver whistle which commanded the winged creatures, instructing them to check their flight and bring the chariot safely to earth. Which they obediently did, with a thump and a bump that rattled every bone in the Paynim's body.

They had landed in a grassy meadow where startled cows, who had been placidly grazing, were now galloping in every direction so as to put as much distance as possible between their plump selves and the two Wyverns. Cows being only cows, they did not realize that Wyverns generally fed only on serpents, toads, scorpions, and the like.

Gaglioffo rubbed the tears from his eyes and looked around curiously, wondering where they were. He saw a small river and a thriving town below the height of the meadow, and, in the distance, surrounded by flowering formal gardens, a stately mansion of considerable age but in fine repair. Walls of hoary stone were overgrown with centuries of ivy; tall casement windows gave forth on the pleasant prospect of farm and field and orchard. It looked very peaceful and serene in the afternoon light.

Just then a cowherd went running by in pursuit of his herd, and Gaglioffo grabbed him by the arm. He waved at the distant mansion. "What place is that?" he inquired.

"Dragonrouge, y'r worship!" declared the cowherd, eyeing the sooty Paynim and his amazing vehicle with disbelief—just before he fainted dead away on the spot.

"Dragonrouge, is it, by Mahoum!" murmured Gaglioffo to himself. "Now where have I heard *that* name before . . .?"

18

Royal Problems in Bohemia

It was less difficult to ride dragon-back than you might think; for one thing, there were ever so many horns and knobs and spines and things to hang onto. It was also more comfortable than you would have expected, for, while the dragon's back was quite hot to the touch, it was broad enough for all three of them. The sheer novelty of the experience more than compensated for what small discomforts there might have been.

They flew across Paflagonia and Pantouflia and Orn, and then across Jaunia, the country of the Yellow Dwarf. And if they did not see the magician Atlantes mounted on Kesrick's faithful Hippogriff, it was probably because the sun was in their eyes at the time.

They arrived at the capital of Bohemia in less time than it would take me to describe their aerial journey—so swift and powerful were the ribbed, membraneous wings of Gartazascus Minor, despite their centuries of disuse—and came to earth in the town square before the royal castle, where pigeons roosted on a bronze memorial statue of the noted chevalier, Astolpho.

The townsfolk gathered at a respectful distance, ogling the Red Dragon but displaying such aplomb that you would have thought dragons were an everyday occurrence hereabouts. Erelong, the King and Queen appeared on a balcony to welcome their visitors, among whom they only recognized Sir Felixmarte. He dismounted and introduced his friends to his would-be father- and mother-in-law.

"Yoo-Hoo, down there! Felixmarte!" called a distant voice. Looking up, they espied a lovely princess floating like a cloud in her skirts and petticoats, neatly and securely tethered to the flagpole atop the tallest turret. A strong, silken rope was tied about her left ankle so that she would not blow away in the breeze. She waved a white lace handkerchief at them

Felixmarte excused himself and entered the castle with alacrity. In no time flat, they saw him leaning out of the highest window with a rolled-up sheet of parchment in one hand which he employed like a megaphone to shout tender greetings and sweet nothings to his blushing but weightless lady-love.

They dismounted and bade farewell to their winged steed, grateful for his assistance. He grinned, displaying rows of teeth like cavalry sabres, and thanked them for severing the admantine chains and releasing him from Durance Vile.

"I would ask you one more favor, dragon, if

you would be so kind," added Kesrick. "I would be much obliged if you did not ramp and ravage either the Kingdom of Bohemia or mine own estates in the Kingdom of the Franks."

"Nothing is further from my mind," the Red Dragon assured him solemnly, crossing his scaly chest just above the heart with a foreclaw. "I am anxious to return at once to Mount Caucausus and see how my draklings have grown and to relieve the anxieties of my dragoness."

He rolled enormous lamplike eyes toward Arimaspia. "I will be forever grateful, mistress, for your kindness and sympathy," he said shyly.

The Scythian Princess smiled with delight and patted him on the head—*carefully,* of course, because of all those spikes and things. Then the enormous creature bade them step back out of the way, spread his opal wings, and soared aloft, circling the spires of the castle and waving good-bye to Sir Felixmarte, before arrowing off into the east and dwindling rapidly from view.

The King of Bohemia was stout and fussy and short of breath and kept whuffling into his side whiskers; Queen Balanice was tall and calm and matronly. They introduced their visitors to some of the court officials, including the Royal Treasurer, Count de Shekels, General Bombastus, the commander of the Bohemian army, Herr Schnipp Barber by Appointment to Their Majesties, and Von Hedzoff, the Royal Executioner.

A buffet meal had hastily been set in the dining room. While they ate and drank they

Royal Problems in Bohemia

discussed the piteous plight of the Princess Lunetta. In the distance, they could hear the faint voice of the love-smitten Hyrcanian knight as he bellowed a sonnet through the megaphone he had contrived.

"He will have a sore throat in no time, if he keeps *that* up, the poor dear!" remarked the Queen, daintily slicing a nectarine with a slim silver fruit knife.

"I say, my boy," huffed King Bardondon, once Sir Kesrick and Arimaspia had given a brief account of their recent adventures, "why couldn't you lift the enchantment on our daughter as you broke the spell on those adamantine chains—that is, with the magical power of the Sword of Undoings." He sounded so hopeful that Kesrick regretted having to dash those hopes.

"Sire, nothing would make me happier than to do so, were it only possible," he declared in noble, ringing tones. "But, alas, the pommelstone of Dastagerd can only reverse or nullify the enchantments of mortal sorcerers. It's no use trying it against *fairy magic*, you see."

"Oh, well," sighed the King dispiritedly.

"Perhaps by this time the wicked fairy has forgiven your unintentional slight to her dignity, and could be coaxed into removing the spell voluntarily," suggested Arimaspia, trying to be helpful. The king shook his head slowly.

"Not *her*," he said bitterly. "Not Dame Concaline, the old hag! She's famous for her grudges; once, for a similar slight, she carried off the Princess Joliette and locked her up for years in a stone tower and treated her harshly, until the unfortunate lass managed to escape from her clutches. No, there's no hope there."

"Well, never you mind, something will occur to Sir Kesrick; it always does," said Arimaspia encouragingly, with a fond glance at her hero.

"I certainly hope so," sighed the King, munching a cherry tart. "Very disconcerting, you know, having one's daughter floating around in the sky half of every month. Certainly lowers the dignity of Royalty in the estimate of the commoners."

"On the other hand," remarked Arimaspia, who was determined to find some good in this malign enchantment, "Princess Lunetta, from her unique vantage, could certainly spy an enemy army bound on invading Bohemia, from leagues away."

The King nodded thoughtfully.

"There is that, m'lady," he agreed. "Why, only last spring she spotted the troops of the Emperor Contalabutte on their way here from up north in plenty of time for stout old Bombastus to put 'em to rout!"

"See? I told you so," exclaimed the Princess of Scythia soothingly.

The visitors were invited to spend the night in the castle and happily accepted.

The next morning they arose bright and early and breakfasted *al fresco* in the gardens. As predicted, Felixmarte had lost his voice from yelling all of those sweet nothings through his paper trumpet, and his throat was so sore that the Queen of Bohemia made him wear a piece of pink flannel tied over it.

"Have another cup of hot tea with honey and lemon, sir knight," the Queen advised him. "It's good for the laryngitis."

Felixmarte, who looked gloomier and more melancholy than usual, even for *him*, nodded politely and croaked, "Thank you, madame," in hoarse, rasping tones.

Just before noontime, more unexpected visitors arrived at the capital, and these were none other than our old friends, Sir Mandricardo the Tartar knight, and his lady-love, the Amazon girl, Callipygia. They had at length given up trying to discover the whereabouts of Kesrick and Arimaspia, and had decided to seek lodgings in the nearest city, which turned out to be the capital of seacoast Bohemia.

You can imagine the exchange of hearty, delighted greetings when the sundered comrades encountered each other: Kesrick slapped Mandricardo on the back and wrung his hand firmly, while Arimaspia and Callipygia embraced and kissed each other on the cheeks. The newcomers were quickly introduced to their royal host and hostess, and also to Sir Felixmarte and even to the Princess Lunetta, who waved her lace hankie from aloft.

"I say, birthday curse, eh?" exclaimed the Tartar knight. "Seem to be havin' a lot more of those down in these parts of the world than I'd imagine. Quite thought the custom had gone out of fashion generations ago, dash it all."

"Wicked fairies can be troublesome," agreed the Amazon girl wisely. "Set me in front of the old hag with my sword at the ready, and we'll see if she doesn't decide to cooperate!"

"Not a bad idear, that," commented Sir Mandricardo interestedly. "Where does this Dame Concaline generally reside, what?"

"She customarily resides in a gloomy cavern up in the hills," said the King of Bohemia, "but, according to the society page in the *Bohemia Morning Bugle,* she's off on a visit to her old friend, the enchanter Grumedan, in the country of Quesiton ... or was it Nacumera?"

"Doesn't much matter," said Sir Mandricardo, heavily. "Both lands are under the dominion of the Emperor Prester John, and *that's* half a world away from here."

"Wasn't it the kingdom of Mataquin, dear?" asked Queen Balanice. Her royal husband shrugged gloomily.

"Getting forgetful in my old age," he grumbled. "But what's the difference if it was? Mataquin's twelve thousand leagues from here ..."

They continued to discuss the problem, but without finding a solution. After a while, Felixmarte went back to his window in the tower. His voice was so hoarse he couldn't shout endearments to the princess, so he had to write them out on large sheets of cardboard and hold them up so that she could read them.

19

Callipygia's Adventure

As it happened, the Queen of Bohemia was perfectly correct in her memory: Dame Concaline was indeed in the kingdom of Mataquin, having flown there from her gloomy cavern high in the hills astride a huge grey Toad equipped with batlike wings. She rode this creature, daintily sitting sidesaddle, with her black skirts rucked up, and whipped it on with a live cobra instead of a riding crop.

She was remarkably ugly, and so old that she only had one eye in her head and one tooth left in her mouth. Fairies can live for ages and ages, as you probably know, and generally—if they are of sweet disposition and have kindly hearts—they remain young and beautiful forever —if they want to, that is. But if they are mean or jealous or spiteful, they become uglier with every foul deed or despicable crime. Which explains why Dame Concaline had a face that would stop a clock.

Her old partner in crime, Grumedan the Enchanter, was no less repulsive than she. If you have not read about him in the histories of the Princess Potentilla, well, suffice it to say that he was very large and fat and clumsy, with long yellow teeth and one eye in the center of his forehead. He also stammered rather badly.

He lived in an enchanted castle, whose approaches were guarded by ferocious lions who were chained like watchdogs. Concaline, of course, flew over the chained lions and landed neatly on one of the parapets of Grumedan's castle. The enchanter came shuffling out to greet his old crony.

"My d-dear Cuk-cuk-Concaline, how ch-ch-charming!" he said, revealing long teeth in a smile of welcome.

"Hrrmph!" replied the old fairy. "Have your lackeys put my Toad in the stables, *if* you please!"

"Suh-suh-certainly, m-madame."

And they sat down to a tasty repast of ragout of viper, jellied worms in aspic and a refreshing salad of wolfbane and aconite. As they gobbled up this disgusting mess, they regaled each other with descriptions of their latest villainies, Concaline cackling with laughter and Grumedan roaring with good humor.

Nothing delights the villainous as much as to hear of the villainies of others.

After breakfast, Callipygia wandered off to the smithy where she intended to oil and polish her armor and accouterments and to sharpen her sword on the whetstone. She found that

Callipygia's Adventures

these tasks had already been taken care of by the armorer, on orders of the king, who was certainly a thoughtful and hospitable monarch. With nothing else to occupy her time, the Amazon girl strolled into the castle's library and read the morning papers. There she discovered that, according to the author of the society news column, the wicked fairy had arrived in Mataquin as the guest of the enchanter Grumedan.

Now, Callipygia was in a bad humor. For one thing, the adventurous Amazon girl had not been the heroine of an adventure for a depressingly long time. While she had passed through innumerable perils, hazards, dangers and vicissitudes, she had not gotten out of any of these because of her own doing, but had been rescued from them by Kesrick or Mandricardo or the sorcerer Pteron, or somebody else. And Amazons, being woman warriors, feel that they can fight and face dangers at least as well as any man.

These thoughts put her into a gloomy frame of mind. While she loved her Tartar knight dearly, she felt that she was not quite holding up her end of their adventures, but leaving everything to him and his friends. Taming the Monoceros she dismissed with a snort: it is in the nature of Monoceroses to be tamed by virgins, and the poor brute was merely obeying its own instincts. She desperately wished to do something so brave and gallant that it would earn her the deepest admiration of Sir Mandricardo.

Now, as it happened, the library of the royal castle was adjoined by the royal museum, wherein the current King of Bohemia and his ancestors kept various curios, mementoes and rarities in glass cases, each exhibit neatly labeled. For a time, Callipygia amused herself by looking at and admiring such treasures as the eggshell of Roc, in a case large enough to have comfortably housed a whale, a golden comb and mirror which had once belonged to the famous mermaid, Melusine, a tiny golden coronet (prettily set with chip diamonds) once worn by the Frog-Prince, the celebrated Glass Slipper (the left one, not the right one) worn by Queen Cinderella I of Pantouflia, and other historical antiquities.

She stopped dead in front of the last case in the museum. It contained a dilapidated pair of high-heeled boots of shabby blue leather, adorned with silver buckles badly in need of polishing. Bending closer, she read the card:

SEVEN-LEAGUE BOOTS (GENUINE)
Believed by Authorities to be the Pair Stolen from the Ogre by Hop-o'-my-Thumb, circa 1697.

The eyes of the Amazon girl sparkled with excitement at this discovery. What did it matter if the Kingdom of Mataquin was twelve thousand leagues away, if one had seven-league boots? (That is, of course, boots that carry their wearer seven leagues at a single stride.) Here was just the mode of transportation Callipygia required to go and beard the wicked fairy in her den—well, in the den of the enchanter Grumedan, anyway!

Callipygia's Adventure

Her mind a busy turmoil of plans and calculations, the Amazon girl opened the case and purloined the famous seven-league boots—scribbling an I.O.U., which she signed and put in the case, so that the custodian would not think the museum had been ransacked by a mere burglar.*

She then re-entered the library and looked up Mataquin in the atlas, to ascertain its precise location. She also took the precaution of looking up the enchanter Grumedan in the *Who's Who*, next briefly visited the castle kitchens on a mysterious errand which I will explain shortly, then donned her mail and gear and weapons, repaired to a long gallery where open casements looked forth on the morning, pulled on the shabby old boots—took one stride—and was gone in a twinkling.

Traveling by seven-league boots turned out to be a most disconcerting experience. One step and you are in a town square; another step, and you find yourself in a forest; a third step, and you might be perched atop a mountain or in the midst of a desert, or on a seashore, or whatever. The rapid and dizzying change of scene made Callipygia giddy; it was rather like switching your tv set from channel to channel very quickly.

Not being of a mathematical mind, the Ama-

---

* Her signature was *Callipygia Fecit.*, which is how Princesses of Royal Blood sign their names. You haven't forgotten that our Callipygia was one of the seventeen daughters of the Queen of Amazonia, have you?

zon girl had not realized how swiftly the seven-league boots would carry her to Mataquin, which journey, by the way, was accomplished in 28 and ½ mintues, but she had, of course, figured out how many strides she must take to cover the distance of twelve thousand leagues (exactly one thousand, seven hundred and fourteen—with a little skip after the last stride, in order to cover the two remaining leagues). She had figured this out, of course, so as not to pass over Mataquin and miss it entirely.

She arrived before Grumedan's castle out of breath, dizzy, and with weary, aching legs. She had not realized how walking in seven-league boots tires the wearer—which she could have found out by reading the works of the historian Perrault; but, then, Callipygia was never much for reading books.

The Amazon girl stripped off the blue leather boots and tucked them by their floppy tops through her girdle, while looking around to reconnoiter. The castle before her, which rose on the barren edges of a desolate waste, was certainly gloomy and grim enough to have afforded a suitable residence for the likes of the enchanter Grumedan, but, for all that Callipygia knew, there might easily be more than one evil enchanter living in the kingdom of Mataquin.

It was the lions chained before the entrance of the castle, blocking every avenue of egress, that convinced her that her unusual footwear had transported her to the exact spot she wished to be. There were at least eighteen lions in view at the moment—and others probably chained around the corner and in the back—

and they were roaring bloodthirstily at the first whiff of the intruder.

Callipygia was a brave and resourceful Amazon, but not quite up to doing battle with eighteen hungry lions. She had envisioned precisely this predicament, and had prepared for it. That is to say, she had asked the King of Bohemia's chef to fix up a quantity of small cakes made out of millet flour, sugar-candy and crocodile eggs. Everyone in Terra Magica knows that such cakes—made from the famous recipe of the Fairy of the Mountain—are a delicacy which lions find irresistible.

With her heart in her mouth, Callipygia began tossing the little cakes to every lion in sight.

In just a few moments she would know whether she had correctly remembered the recipe.

20

Atlantes Solves a Mystery

The royal castle of Bohemia was in an uproar about lunchtime, when it was discovered that Callipygia was mysteriously missing. Pageboys were sent scampering to search every attic, apartment, suite and corridor, while the grooms hunted for her in the stables, the cooks in the kitchens, the gardeners in the palace grounds, and so on and so forth. Nowhere was the Amazon girl to be found.

It was a puzzle! Wherever could she have gotten to? Sir Mandricardo fretted and fumed.

"Quite unlike the lass, what?" he demanded resentfully. "Goin' off like this, without a word to *anybody!* Might have fallen down the well, or something—"

"We looked there," murmured the King.

"We have looked everywhere," wailed the Queen, wringing her hands. What this would do to damage the reputation of the royal hospitality of Bohemia was beyond reckoning

Atlantes Solves a Mystery

"The cellars—"

"There, too," said the King.

"The pigeon-loft—"

Kesrick blinked at that one.

"Oh, come now, friend! What in the *world* would your lady-love be doing in the pigeon-loft?" he demanded.

"Anyway, we looked there," said King Bardondon.

"Well, she ain't gone ridin'—not a horse missing from the stables," mused Sir Mandricardo, frowning in angry bafflement.

"Wherever dear Callipygia went, she took her mail and weapons with her," Arimaspia pointed out worriedly. "She must have been anticipating some sort of danger—"

In case you're wondering, yes, the pages looked in the library *and* the castle museum. But they were looking for a tall lady of rather ample proportions, not checking to see if any of the treasures of the museum were missing, which explains why it was not until considerably later that the purloining of the famous seven-league boots was discovered.

It was certainly a mystery, and puzzled and worried them all. At least until the arrival of the famous Wizard of the Pyrénées.

Atlantes came flying in just in the middle of lunch, astride the Hippogriff, which whinnyed and croaked with delight at seeing his long-lost, strayed or stolen master, Kesrick. The old wizard climbed stiffly down from the saddle, his long white beard thrusting out from the open face of his sparkling steel helmet, beaming affably at everybody in sight.

"There you are, young Kesrick!" he chortled. "Well, now, somebody—anybody!—help me out of this hot, heavy armor before I stifle, and give me something cold to drink, I pray you, and I'll tell you what has been happening."

This was soon accomplished, and the young Frankish knight was delighted and proud that his faithful steed had possessed the presence of mind to fly home to the stables of the Iron Castle in the Pyrénées when he had gotten lost. The creature seemed none the worse for his perils.

Cackling good-humoredly, Atlantes was interested and amused to learn how they had escaped from the clutches of the Giant Thunderthighs, and to hear of their other travels and exploits. Learning that Dame Callipygia was mysteriously missing, his face grew long and solemn, and his eyes thoughtful.

"Well, now, 'pon my word! That is a mystery," he said slowly. "Wench ever do anything like this before?"

"Never!" declared Sir Mandricardo.

"Gone off to have an adventure of her own, perchance?" cleverly guessed the shrewd old sorcerer.

"On foot?" demanded the Tartar knight.

"Hmm. Hem. Hrrmph!" said Atlantes, thinking deeply. "Well, there are other means of traveling about the country, you know! Flying carpets; seven-league boots; the famous clockwork Magic Horse belonging to the King of

Atlantes Solves a Mystery

Delhi, but now in the possession of my old friend, Pteron—"

"We've a pair of seven-league boots right here!" remarked the King of Bohemia in surprised tones.

"Is that so?" inquired Atlantes. "Where d'ye keep 'em?"

"Why, in the castle's museum, right next door to the library . . ."

"Better send somebody to see if they're still there," suggested Atlantes. "Madame, could I beg another slice of that excellent cheese?"

A page was dispatched, and soon came scampering back, eyes wide with excitement, brandishing Callipygia's note. They read it with a mingling of emotions in which exasperation, relief, curiosity and mystification might be counted.

"Well, I'll be—!" solemnly declared the King.

"Another mystery solved—if I do say so meself," cackled the old wizard with extreme satisfaction. "Pass the port."

While these events had been taking place, Kesrick's fairy godmother was still searching the length and breadth of Terra Magica for some sign of her favorite godson. And Dame Pirouetta (who seldom listed Patience among her many virtues) was becoming heartily exasperated.

Her glittering and magical Cloud had already traversed the famous Kingdom of China and the dominions of the Grand Cham, to say nothing of the Empire of Prester John, without discovering the slightest trace of Sir Kesrick. Erelong she had explored Amazonia, Hindoostan, Persia, the Empire of Tartary, and even Scythia, and what little amount of patience the old Fairy of the Fountain did possess was completely exhausted.

"Where can that red-headed young rascal have possibly gotten to?" she wondered to herself, soaring over Pamphyllia, Pantouflia and Crim-Tartary. And, indeed, the Knight of Dragonrouge seemed to have completely vanished from the knowledge of men. Or fairies!

"Perchance the wise Atlantes has enjoyed better luck on his quest than have I on mine," she fumed, tapping one foot impatiently on her Cloud. She was well aware that the Wizard of the Pyrénées intended to visit the royal capital of seacoast Bohemia, for he had informed her of his plans during their last conference. And, as that country and Hyrcania lay not very far to the west, Dame Pirouetta determined to discover if Atlantes had yet reached King Bardondon's capital.

Even powerful fairies like Dame Pirouetta aren't aware of everything that is happening in the wide-wayed world. Had she thought to bring with her the enchanted looking-glass, Sir Kesrick's fairy godmother could have located his whereabouts in mere instants. But you simply can't think of *everything* when you are hurriedly packing for an unexpected journey.

Indeed, Dame Pirouetta had half a notion to steer her Cloud directly home to the fountain amid the green glades of the forest of Broceliande, where she could consult the magic looking-glass.

But seacoast Bohemia was in the same direc-

tion, and much nearer than the enchanted forest in Brittany, so she remained firm in her
resolve to visit the capital first and see if the
wise old Wizard of the Pyrénées had found out
anything about the whereabouts of Kesrick of
Dragonrouge.

But she was irritated at her own thought-
lessness. She could easily have stuffed the magic
looking-glass into her reticule if it had occurred
to her to do so. The mirror could be made
small enough to fit in the jeweled reticule beside the small stone bottle of water from the
Fountain of Lions, her diamond-studded com-
pact and lace handkerchief and powder-puff
and rouge-pot and platinum comb, and all of
the other articles therein.

But even fairy godmothers cannot envision
every contingency that may arise on an adventure like this one . . . and it had been centuries
since she had last visited the dominions of the
Grand Cham, and it had been pleasant to have
rosewater tea with her old friend, and King of
Delhi, down in Hindoostan.

The sparkling Cloud rolled on through the
afternoon skies toward the capital of King
Bardondon and Queen Balanice, making excellent time due to a brisk tail-wind.

How astonished would Dame Pirouetta have
been could she have guessed the surprises that
awaited her in seacoast Bohemia!

BOOK FIVE

DISENCHANTING LUNETTA

21

In Grumedan's Castle

Luckily for Callipygia, her memory proved accurate, and the old recipe for lion-pacifying cakes which the Fairy of the Mountain had long ago divulged to the mother of Princess Bellissima, and which she used to pass the lions that guarded the abode of the Fairy of the Desert, retained its famous potency.

The eighteen lions ceased their roaring the instant the Amazon girl began tossing the cakes she had ordered from the kitchens of King Bardondon. They flung themselves upon these tasty morsels and gobbled them up greedily. Whereupon they became as tame as tabby-cats. In fact, the one nearest to where Callipygia stood in trepidation rolled over on its back with its paws in the air as if it desired to have its tummy rubbed. Which Callipygia did, somewhat gingerly, with the toe of her sandal.

Then she simply walked through the row of tame lions and entered the grim portals of the castle of the enchanter Grumedan. The interior was every bit as gloomy and sinister as the outside had been, and perhaps even more so. Human skulls were piled in the corners of the great hall, and coffins of wood or stone (the latter carven all over with Egyptian hieroglyphics, which the brave Amazon girl could not read) stood leaning against the damp and dripping walls—for Grumedan was something of a necromancer, as well as being an enchanter.

The great hall was rather like a forest, its high-domed roof supported by stone pillars rough-hewn as tree trunks. Callipygia wove her silent way among them, keeping well into the shadows. And discovered the enchanter Grumedan still at table with his guest, the wicked fairy.

They had just finished a salad of stinging-nettles, and were working away at bottle after bottle of deadly hemlock. Lurking prudently in the shadow of the stone pillars, the Amazon girl tried to eavesdrop on their conversation. Alas, it was in Chaldaean, a language much favored by wicked fairies and evil enchanters, and one with which Callipygia was unfamiliar.

The two were discussing their most recent villainies and betrayals, and they sniggered nastily over the vile details of these, but Callipygia, not understanding the language, derived naught therefrom.

The impetuous Amazon girl would have flung herself upon both of these sorcerous villains, but a shred or two of prudence warned her otherwise. The brave warrior-woman had planned to confront Concaline with her blade—but the presence of the evil enchanter made her change her mind. Callipygia was about as courageous as a woman may be, but to challenge *both* a wicked fairy and an evil enchanter at the same time seemed foolhardy.

And Callipygia, however reckless, was certainly no fool. So she lurked in the shadows, and listened, and waited for the time to be ripe for her to strike.

A stumbling cadaver, his hips and nose fretted by the bites of many maggots, entered, deposited on the table (which was, by the way, of rotten gallows-wood) another brace of bottles of the fine hemlock, and staggered stiffly away.

Grumedan and his guest were getting royally drunk, as the saying goes. Their conversation strayed from Chaldaean to High Inca, then to the forgotten Senzar language of Lost Atlantis. They giggled and chortled over each others' most recent iniquities, and all the while, Callipygia listened impatiently.

Neither of the two cronies could possibly have seen her as she stood in the shadows. The only illumination in Grumedan's hall was a fire of wizardry which flickered on the grate, its sinister green and yellow flames sizzling and popping.

After a while, the two feasters began to nod off. Grumedan laid his immense ugly head in an empty bowl of scorpion soup, and his one eye closed in drunken slumber. As for Concaline, she had taken aboard more than a bottle or two too many of the fine vintage hemlock: laying her ugly face in the remnants of the stinging-nettle salad, she began to snore with all the resonance of a buzz-saw cutting through a log of seasoned mahogany.

Callipygia realized that the time was ripe for her to exert herself. Heaven alone could fortell just how long the ugly twain would slumber, and anyway, she was only interested in the wicked fairy.

She crept stealthily from the shadows and approached the long table of maggoty gallows-wood. The only illumination in Grumedan's great hall came from the wizardly fire on the grate; all else was inky, leaping shadows.

Affixed by iron chains to many of the stone pillars were the gnawed skeletons of men and women. With swift and skillful hands, the Amazon girl detached a few of these chains, letting their bony burdens clatter to the floor. She caught up the light body of the wicked fairy Concaline in her strong arms, and bound her in these borrowed chains. The one-eyed and one-toothed fairy snored on, oblivious of capture.

It was but the matter of a moment for Callipygia to put on the seven-league boots she had borrowed from the museum of King Bardondon. Then, tossing the light, bony burden of the drunken fairy across her strong shoulders, she stepped through the long casement windows of Grumedan's castle, gained the parapet, and began her journey back to Bohemia.

Concaline snored lustily all the way across the world.

They were strolling in the gardens of King Bardondon's palace discussing Lunetta's prob-

In Grumedan's Castle

lem, when a glittering Cloud appeared with an elderly grand-dame riding thereupon, handsomely attired in clothing which had been out of fashion for ages. It was, of course, Dame Pirouetta and they were all delighted to see her, except perhaps for Sir Felixmarte, who jumped nervously at the unexpected apparition, for he had never met the lady before.

Grinning happily, Kesrick strode to the edge of the Cloud to help his godmother dismount. She gave a haughty sniff at the sight of him and her wrinkled features assumed an expression of severe disapproval, although secretly she was quite pleased to find him alive and seemingly unharmed.

"There you are, you mischievous young rascal!" exclaimed Dame Pirouetta. "And a merry chase you've led me, I'm sure. Hither, thither and yon I've been this morning, and nary a sign of you could I discover."

He smiled at her so charmingly that her heart melted with affection, and she deigned to accept his assistance in dismounting and even permitted him to kiss her powdered cheek.

Kesrick explained about the dragon and how they had eluded the Giant Thunderthighs, and so on. He also introduced his fairy godmother to Felixmarte and to the tiny figure of the enchanted princess who was, as usual, floating about far above. She waved her handkerchief in greeting.

King Bardondon bowed profoundly to the fairy and expressed delight at being able to welcome her to his palace. Queen Balanice curtsied gracefully and murmured some polite social amenity or other, but privately she wondered how many more unexpected visitors might be arriving. Dame Pirouetta made Number Seven, and if this kept up they would shortly be running out of guest rooms in the palace and would have to put some of them up in the local inn.

Dame Pirouetta greeted them shortly, and permitted her old friend Atlantes to kiss her bejeweled hand. Then she listened with interest and approval as they told her a brief account of their adventures and, in particular, the problems of Princess Lunetta.

"Poor gel!" murmured Kesrick's fairy godmother. "It must be most uncomfortable for a body to just float about, shooing off the pigeons and praying that it don't rain. That wicked Concaline! She'll get her come-uppance one day quite soon, I promise you! I'll have her up on charges before Queen Paridamie"—that was the name of the Queen of the Fairies here in Bohemia—"before she knows what's happening."

"Pray tell us, madame, do you think there is anything at all you can do to help our unfortunate daughter in her present difficulties?" inquired King Bardondon.

"Oh, yes, madame—can you break or dissolve the enchantment?" asked Queen Balanice.

"Mebbe so; mebbe no," mused Pirouetta thoughtfully. "Never, since the world was a world, has there been a spell that couldn't be broken, some way or other. I'll think on't, my good woman."

They were about to troop in to lunch, with

In Grumedan's Castle

the Queen hurrying ahead to inform the butler that there would be one more place at table, when suddenly Callipygia appeared, red in the face and slightly out of breath, with a curious, snoring bundle over her shoulder.

This made Felixmarte jump nervously again. If there were going to be any more of these sudden and magical appearances of people out of nowhere, his nerves would be in a sorry state.

The Amazon girl dumped her bundle on the grass and sat down to pull off the seven-league boots, relieved to be finished with them. On the whole, they formed a disconcerting—even an alarming—mode of transportation.

22

Grumedan to the Rescue

When the enchanter Grumedan awoke from his
little snooze and discovered his guest nowhere
on the premises, he was not at first concerned.
He assumed that Concaline had simply gone
upstairs to the guest room for a nap. When he
found that room unoccupied he began to worry.

"Wh-where *has* the old hah-hah-harridan gotten to?" he grumbled pettishly. As there is little sense in being an enchanter *and* a necromancer if you can't find out what happened
while you were asleep, he soon solved the mystery of the vanishing fairy.

"Oh, duh-duh-drat the bothersome hag!" he
exclaimed, displaying little of the concern a
host should properly feel when a house guest
has been carried off right under one's nose.
The fact of the matter is that while Grumedan
and Concaline were old cronies and partners in
villainy, there was little love lost between them,

Grumedan to the Rescue

for both were wicked and treacherous and each knew the other to be so.

He did, however, resolve to fly to Bohemia to rescue her. But his was a much more practical and self-serving motive merely than friendly concern for the well-being of the ugly old fairy.

That is, since Concaline was privy to all of his secret plots and plans and villainies, she might well under duress divulge this information to her captors. And about the very last thing any evil enchanter desires is to have his enemies find out the schemes he has against them—especially since more than a few of the hapless victims of Grumedan's enchantments were not even aware of his existence.

He therefore donned traveling-clothes and slipped the Ring of Gyges on his plump right forefinger (which made him completely invisible). Then he climbed aboard Concaline's bat-winged flying Toad, spurred it aloft, and headed in the direction of Bohemia.

It would seem that Queen Balanice had been perfectly correct in worrying about another unexpected guest.

Back in Bohemia, Concaline was rudely roused from her nap by being doused with a bucket of water from the nearest fountain. Spluttering groggily, she blinked about with her one bleary eye, discovering herself a captive. This did nothing to improve her temper, as you might imagine.

She snapped her bony fingers and the chains which bound her fell apart, link by link.

She did not recognize Atlantes, never having

heretofore encountered the elderly gentleman, but she knew Pirouetta at a glance and was not in the least daunted by her.

"Well!" she snapped, fuming. "Here's a fine kettle of fish, I must say! Snatching a body from her rest without so much as a by-yer-leave! I've a good mind to turn the lot of you into toads . . .!"

"You'll do nothing of the sort, madame, or I'll give you nine more fat warts on your ugly nose," retorted Pirouetta sternly.

Concaline cackled evilly. "Warts, is it? We'll see about that. And what, pray tell, does yer high-and-mightiness want with me?"

"We seek the removal of your enchantment from Princess Lunetta," said Sir Kesrick. The wicked old fairy shot him a malevolent glance.

"And why should I?" she demanded with a gloating leer which exposed the one fang which remained in her withered gums. She cast a glance at the enchanted princess who was still floating around above the tallest spire of the castle. "Makes a fine birdie, she does. Anyway, moon's changin' toward the full and she'll be comin' down presently."

"Dame Pirouetta, can't you simply break the enchantment with your own fairy magic?" inquired the Scythian Princess. Kersick's fairy godmother shook her head reluctantly.

"A birthday curse is a birthday curse, and under the Laws of Faerie, Dame Concaline was entitled to one, if only out of spite for not being invited to the party," she explained.

"I say, bit of an impasse, what?" murmured

Grumedan to the Rescue

Mandricardo to Sir Felixmarte, who sighed and looked wretched.

It was at this juncture that the young knight of Hyrcania happened to remember the words which Friar Althotas had given to them in parting: "Two ills can sometimes make a cure." At the time, Felixmarte had made nothing out of the enigmatic phrase; nor could he now, but he repeated it aloud.

Pirouetta looked thoughtful.

"Let me think; let me think," she murmured distractedly.

Grumedan's flying Toad made nowhere near as good time in traversing the twelve thousand leagues as Callipygia's seven-league boots had done, but he nonetheless arrived at the palace of King Bardondon and Queen Balanice eventually.

Unseen by any, due to the Ring of Gyges which he wore upon his finger, the enchanter brought the winged Toad to a landing on the lawn of the palace, and sat silent and still in order to study the situation. The presence of the two knights and the Amazon girl didn't bother him a trifle, but the fact that the old Wizard of the Pyrénées was there, to say nothing of the potent and powerful fairy, Dame Pirouetta, did make him cautious.

He prudently resolved, therefore, to bide his time and wait for an opportunity to snatch Concaline from their midst. A well-timed diversion might do the trick, if he could only think of one that would work. So he silently squatted on toadback and awaited his opportunity.

"An' it's no use yer threatenin' me with that upstart Paridamie, either," Concaline was saying at the moment to Pirouetta. "When the hussy was elected Queen of the Fairies hereabouts, they chose the wench over me own choice, the fairy Surcantine, so they's no love between us— and even th' Queen o' th' Fairies can't force a body to remove a birthday curse."

"Tell me something I don't know," said Dame Pirouetta grimly. She was still deep in thought, and the outlines of a solution to poor Lunetta's problem was beginning to form in her clever mind.

"As I've said, the laws which cover birthday curses are very precise," said Kesrick's fairy godmother slowly. "However, since I also was not invited to the party, fairy law entitles me to a birthday curse as well as Concaline."

"Oh, my," murmured King Bardondon nervously. "I do hope you won't do that, madame! Lunetta's mother and meself didn't invite you because we didn't know you were even in Bohemia at the time."

"As it happens, I was. Just a brief visit to obtain a bottle of water from the celebrated Fountain of Lions. At the time, I took no exception to not being invited, as no one knew I was anywhere near. But now I intend to pronounce my own curse on your unfortunate daughter—"

They all looked apprehensive, not counting Dame Concaline, who looked baffled and confused. Dame Pirouetta turned to confront the wicked fairy.

"I gather that your curse on the princess was something-or-other to the effect that 'as the moon

Grumedan to the Rescue

wanes, so shall her weight,' am I correct in my assumption?"

"That's as it may be," mumbled Concaline warily.

"Well, madame, was it or was it not?" snapped Pirouetta tartly.

"That's fer me to know and yerself to find out," said the wicked fairy. Pirouetta shrugged. "Well, it doesn't really matter." She pointed her fairy wand toward the sky where, at present, the enchanted princess was trying to shoo away a flock of crows. First, of course, she jiggled the magic wand to make the diamonds which composed its star-tip begin sparkling and flashing with power.

Then she slowly and emphatically bestowed her own birthday curse on Lunetta.

"As—the—moon—wanes—her—weight— shall—wax."

There was dead silence. They gazed at one another wordlessly, and then with one accord turned to stare aloft with hopeful eyes.

23

Consequences of a Double Enchantment

As lightly as a falling leaf, Princess Lunetta began to float down toward the ground. Her skirts and petticoats billowing about her ankles in a froth of snowy lace, an expression of delight and amazement on her pretty face, she clapped both hands to her head to hold her coronet in place.

It was obvious that she was recovering her normal weight gradually, and they all realized that the curse of weightlessness had been cancelled by the curse of weightfulness, and that if Dame Pirouetta's fairy magic was done adeptly (which, of course, it was), Lunetta should suffer no discomforts during the lunar phases. In a word, her weight was and would remain precisely normal.

"Unfair!" wailed Concaline in a shrill screech. It grieved her hard old heart to see one of her most malevolent enchantments so cleverly undone.

Consequences of a Double Enchantment

"Not at all, madame," sniffed Pirouetta, feeling very satisfied and pleased with herself. Then she turned to receive the thanks of the grateful King and Queen of Bohemia, who were anxiously awaiting their daughter's return to earth.

"What a clever idea," marveled Arimaspia. "However did you think of it, madame?"

The old fairy smiled slightly. "Actually, it was due to a remark by this young gentleman," she admitted, pointing with her wand to Felixmarte "That quotation which the good Friar gave you when you sundered your companionship . . ."

"You refer to the passage 'Two ills can sometimes make a cure'?" said the Hyrcanian knight. Pirouetta nodded.

"Quite so; when you remembered the passage, sir, it suddenly occurred to me that if I couldn't break Concaline's enchantment, I could at least negate it with an opposite enchantment. Methinks, sir, that the good Friar you encountered in the woods was a better friend than you ever expected!"

By this time, Princess Lunetta had descended and now, as they broke off their conversation, she settled gracefully to earth, landing in a flower bed.

Her father embraced her; her mother kissed her rosy lips; and, as for Sir Felixmarte, the lovesick young knight from Hyrcania threw himself at her feet with a thousand fervent protestations of his tender feelings.

His ardent words brought a blush to her maidenly cheeks, but her eyes gazed upon him fondly. Demurely, she permitted him to kiss

Consequences of a Double Enchantment

her hand—something he had heretofore only been able to do when the moon was full—and to assist her to step lightly from amid the blossoms. She curtsied humbly before Dame Pirouetta, who gave her a little pat.

"Nonsense, my gel! Not another word! 'Pon my honor as a fairy, it was a positive pleasure to undo the wicked enchantment so cruelly and unfairly bestowed upon you by one whose wicked deeds have earned her many punishments—"

While their attention was distracted from Dame Concaline by the arrival of Princess Lunetta, none of those present gave another thought to the wicked fairy. All, that is, save for the enchanter Grumedan, still squatting a-toadback and as invisible to their eyes as was the breeze itself.

He rightly guessed that *this* was his best opportunity to snatch Concaline from her captors, while they were all greeting the disenchanted Princess, and complimenting her upon the happy occasion of her disenchantment.

Seizing the moment, he sprang from his seat on the saddle of the flying Toad and caught up the bony frame of Concaline, who squawked in alarm and kicked her bony old legs, not understanding what was happening to her. As she struggled, the Ring of Gyges slipped from Grumedan's finger, and the large, clumsy form of the evil enchanter melted clearly into view— causing Felixmarte to jump nervously for a *third* time that morning

When the others turned to discover the cause

of this commotion, they were struck dumb with amazement at the unexpected sight of Grumedan, who had the wicked fairy tucked up under one arm and was just turning about to flee.

Now, as it happened, Mandricardo was the closest of them all to where Grumedan was standing. Instantly realizing that one of her confederates was trying to steal Concaline away from under, as it were, their very noses, the gallant Tartar knight whipped out his trusty sword and bellowed a challenge at the enchanter.

Grumedan didn't have time to argue the matter. He aimed his wand at Sir Mandricardo and uttered a powerful and potent Word: the sky instantly darkened, then the darkness was split asunder by a flash of lightning that felled the Tartar knight and dazzled them all.

Snatching up the Ring of Gyges and jamming it back upon his pudgy finger, Grumedan leaped back on his Toad again. Promptly disappearing from view, both Toad and enchanter, to say nothing of the wicked fairy, flew into the sky and headed back across the twelve thousand leagues between Bohemia and Mataquin as swiftly as was possible.

Leaving a scene of such consternation and alarm behind them as I give my readers freedom to imagine for themselves.

The distinguished author of the *True and Veritable History of the Knight of Dragonrouge* sagely comments, at this point in our narrative, that so often in this life one is plucked from the heights of joy only to be dashed into the

Consequences of a Double Enchantment

depths of despair. This is certainly as true in Terra Cognita as it is in Terra Magica.

One moment they were happily complimenting Princess Lunetta on her disenchantment—the next, they stared with horror and disbelief at the prone body of Sir Mandricardo, laid out stiff as a board on the smoking greensward. Atlantes knelt stiffly to examine the corpse of the Tartar knight, and solemnly pronounced him dead as the proverbial doornail.

Kesrick was stricken to the heart: they had been companions in peril and adventure for so long a time, that he considered Mandricardo his staunchest friend and ally, and could scarcely envision the remainder of this journey without the bluff and hearty Tartar at his side.

Callipygia, of course, was heartbroken. She bit her underlip to choke back her tears, for it is considered unseemly, among Amazons, to give vent to womanly tears. Arimaspia embraced her and sought the words to console her.

As for King Bardondon and Queen Balanice, they were dreadfully upset. It simply *was not done*, in royal circles, to have a house-guest struck down dead by wicked enchanters brandishing thunderbolts. A few more such occurrences could easily give the Kingdom of Bohemia a bad name.

Atlantes turned to Dame Pirouetta, who stood mute with anger and astonishment at this horrible turn of events.

"I suppose, madame, that you are as helpless as am I to reverse this unfortunate happenstance?" he murmured, without much hope in his voice.

Consequences of a Double Enchantment

The Fairy of the Fountain looked grim, thin lips tightly pressed together and fire in her eye.

"That Grumedan shall someday soon pay the price for his innumerable villainies," she said between clenched teeth. "I shall personally lodge a protest with the Fairy Queen at this despicable outrage! Doubtless my old gossip, the fairy Melinette—who looks after affairs in Mataquin and the several parts of Asia—will see the wretch receives the miserable end which he so richly deserves."

She was truly in a towering fury: Grumedan must have realized that the valiant Tartar knight had been under her protection, if only because he was the best friend of her favorite godson. It was for deeds such as this, that the enchanter Grumedan was strictly excluded from the company of sorcerers in general, and could only consort with the likes of Dame Concaline.

Then, rousing herself from her rage, and collecting her wits, she turned to the Wizard of the Pyrénées.

"I would make reply to your question, sir wizard, but actions speak louder than words. Has anyone seen my reticule? I may have left it on my Cloud."

Atlantes looked puzzled, but hastened to comply with the fairy's request.

"I shall be glad to find it for you, madame," said the old wizard, and turned to search the upper works of the glittering Cloud, which had remained stationary ever since Pirouetta had dismounted from it.

24

Reviving Mandricardo

The richly-jeweled reticule was quickly found and placed in the fairy's hands. She snapped it open and removed a stone bottle therefrom. Cut into one side of this article was a legend which read:

AQVA. DE. FONTE. LEONVM.

Which meant, of course, in the Vulgar tongue, "Water from the Fountain of Lions." And everybody present instantly realized what *that* meant and took a respectful step or two backwards and fell into a tense, expectant silence as Dame Pirouetta began to uncork the stone bottle.

Now, in the first place, the Fairy of the Fountain had brought the stone bottle along with her on this journey because the bottle was empty, and she thought it likely that she would, in her peregrinations, pass near enough to the location of the celebrated fountain to refill it.

Reviving Mandricardo

Which is exactly what had happened. During her travels across Terra Magica, when she had been flying back and forth hoping to find Kesrick, she did make a brief side trip to the Fountain and had refilled the stone bottle with the precious Water of Life, prudently careful to fill the bottle and begone from the courtyard of the enchanted palace before twelve o'clock, for otherwise the gates would have closed, thus locking her in

(She had, of course, known enough about the Fountain to make certain she brought with her the required iron rod and two loaves of bread. But this goes without saying.)*

Standing over the corpse of the Tartar knight, Dame Pirouetta sprinkled the body with the magical water. Mandricardo blinked, yawned, stretched his arms, and looked about him.

"I say, dash it all, bad manners to take a nap with company about, what? Beg your pardon, one and all. What *would* the Pater say!"

King Bardondon, Queen Balanice, and Felixmarte and his princess were pale and round-eyed. It is one thing to know how swiftly the celebrated Water of Life works, but quite another thing to see the stuff in action.

As for Callipygia, her relief was so great that

---

* If my readers should ever happen to find themselves in the vicinity of the enchanted castle, let me advise the same precautions. With the iron rod you are supposed to strike the castle gates three times before they will open to give you entry. Two ferocious enchanted lions will approach you, but if you throw each of them one of the loaves of bread, they will do you no harm. And be sure you are gone before it strikes twelve!

she fainted on the spot. Fortunately, the green-sward was thick and lush enough to break her fall, or she might have done herself an injury. (*The True and Veritable History* remarks, at this juncture, that while Amazon girls are not supposed to weep, it seems that they can faint as easily as the rest of their sex.)

It took quite a lot of explaining before the bewildered Sir Mandricardo fully appreciated the fact that Concaline had been rescued by the enchanter Grumedan and that he (meaning Mandricardo) had been struck stone dead by a thunderbolt and would still have been in that condition, had not Dame Pirouetta revived him with the magical Water.

The situation was a new one for Mandricardo, as you might well suppose, and he sought to find the appropriate words to thank the good-hearted fairy.

"I say, madame, 'pon my soul, dash it all, I mean, that is, you know . . . what?" was his feeble attempt at so-doing.

"Not at all, young man, I'm sure. Happy to have been in the position to supply the requisite sort of first aid," said Pirouetta briskly.

"Well, yes, *rawther* . . . but, you know, after all, I mean," he stuttered and stammered, quite red in the face.

"Not another word, mind!" commanded Pirouetta. It quite embarrassed her to be thanked for doing the sort of nice things which good fairies are employed to do anyway.

There had been *quite* enough surprises for one day, so they all went into the castle and

Reviving Mandricardo

enjoyed a splendid and very merry and festive late lunch.

That very afternoon, Sir Felixmarte and Princess Lunetta were married by the palace chaplain. If their nuptials seem a bit hastily contrived to my reader, well, the lovers had been sundered far too long by the unfortunate fact of Lunetta's enchantment, and, anyway, she had used all of those years to prepare her trouseau, which was long since finished twice over. Also, perhaps Felixmarte was anxious to tie the knot before something else Unexpected chanced to occur.

The only other guests besides our friends who were present at the solemnities, were Lunetta's older sister, Princess Rosanella, and her husband, Prince Miriflor. The Fairy of the Fountain was happy to transport these two by her Cloud, so that they could serve as best man and maid of honor.

Queen Balanice cried so many tears at the ceremony that she quite used up eleven lace handkerchiefs, but they were tears of happiness, and, anyway, mothers are supposed to cry at their daughters' weddings.

That evening, after a light supper, the newly-weds departed on their honeymoon. They had decided to visit the Riviera, for the season was perfect, and Dame Pirouetta promised to make sure the weather did not interfere.

King Bardondon had tentatively suggested a trip to the Alps, for the Alpine skiing season had just started. Recalling his grueling ordeal in Thunderthighs' enormous house atop one of those same Alps, Sir Felixmarte shuddered and turned pale, and hastily decided on the seacoast instead.

Incidentally, as for the wicked fairy Concaline and the enchanter Grumedan, those unsavory rascals were never seen or heard from in Bohemia again. It is strongly doubted by the more eminent historians of the period whether the pair got married to each other, partners in crime or not. For one thing, the enchanter Grumedan was about to fall madly in love with Queen Frivola's daughter, the Princess Potentilla, whom he would woo with a not surprising lack of success, until put out of his misery by the fairy Melinette—just as Dame Pirouetta had predicted.

The next day, our friends discussed their plans. Atlantes was eager to return to his enchanted Iron Castle atop the tallest of the Pyrénées, and Dame Pirouetta had been absent too long from her fairy palace beneath the fountain-pool in the Forest of Brociliande.

Sir Mandricardo and the Amazon girl decided to help escort Kesrick and Arimaspia back to Dragonrouge, and were anxious to attend their wedding once they were safe home. As these parts of seacoast Bohemia were not far from Dragonrouge in the Kingdom of the Franks, the trip should be a swift and easy one.

The fairy Pirouetta, however, said No.

"What codswallop is this!" exclaimed that personage, indignantly. "Broceliande is in much the same direction, and, as I am going there meself, why in the world would you wish to

Reviving Mandricardo

travel overland? My Cloud can easily be ex-
panded to accommodate us all."

And so it was decided.

That very afternoon Kesrick, Arimaspia, Mandricardo and Callipygia, as well as Atlantes,
mounted the Cloud, together with Bayardetto
and Brigadore. They bade a fond adieu to King
Bardondon and Queen Balanice, and once these
farewells were completed, Dame Pirouetta commanded her cloud to conduct them straight-
away to Dragonrouge.

Bayardetto fretted and fussed a little, not, of
course, being accustomed to flight through the
skies. Brigadore, however, remained placid and
calm: with his powerful wings, flight was
natural; being *flown* by someone or something
else was, as it chanced, a novel experience, but
the Hippogriff took it in his stride.

Seacoast Bohemia receded rapidly into the
distance. The sun was westering, but the sky
remained light enough for them to stare interestedly over the margins of Dame Pirouetta's
Cloud, looking down at fields and farms and
forests, towns and highways and hamlets, as
these passed swiftly beneath their keel (so to
speak).

In this manner, they passed over the immensity of Bohemia, and over the southerly parts of
Hyrcania, and entered the famous Kingdom of
the Franks.

25

Via Cloud

As none of the travelers, saving for Kesrick and Dame Pirouetta, had ever visited the Frankish kingdom before, Kesrick politely pointed out such sites of interest as Charlemagne's famous capital and named the several provinces over-which they soared.

They flew over Poictesme, and Neustria, and Trypheme. They soared over fields and forests, towns and cities, sparkling rivers and level plains. Frankland was, at that period, one of the more advanced of the kingdoms of the West, and they saw windmills and man-made canals and other modern wonders of science.

"I do trust that, after your travels and adventures, Sir Kesrick, you and your lady will be settling down to the raising of rich crops and fat babies," remarked Dame Pirouetta.

"Madame, you have my most earnest assurance upon that very point," affirmed the Frankish knight, cuddling his lady-love with one

Via Cloud

strong arm. "I can foresee no reason ever to leave my ancestral estate again," he added. While the journeys and hazards he had endured over the past few weeks had been exhilarating, there is, after all, no place like home.

"I am delighted to hear it," said the Fairy of the Fountain with a heartfelt sigh. "Now, perhaps, I can get back to my work and quit zooming about the wide-wayed world effecting your rescue."

"Dame Pirouetta, I promise you that I shall see my husband stays safely at home," added Arimaspia demurely.

Kesrick's fairy godmother smiled at the Scythian Princess but said nothing

They flew on, supported by the Cloud. They traversed the breadth of the great province of Averoigne, and over the small state of Joiry, continuing their journey into the world's west. Twilight began to drag the shadows of tall trees across fertile fields.

"Demmed interestin', what? Flyin', I mean," remarked Sir Mandricardo. "One gets around so much faster, you know. Have to introduce the custom back in Tartary, my gel, once we get home," he confided to Callipygia. She nodded, saying nothing, quite entranced by the spectacular aerial view.

They flew over rivers and cities and towns and mountains which may not be found on any of our maps of France, here in the Lands We Know. Eventually, along toward sunset, they came to earth near Dragonrouge.

"Oh, I say! Jolly good, what?" chortled Sir Mandricardo, seeing at last Kesrick's ancestral home. It was, indeed, a splendid sight: hoary walls of ancient stone draped with tapestries of ivy, long casement windows opening upon the prospect of velvety lawns and rose gardens, and cozy nooks and splashing fountains. If not exactly a palace, it was at very least a sumptuous and handsome country villa . . . the sort of home to which every prince and princess in a fairy tale should return at the happy ending.

There were fields and farms and grape arbors; small pebbly paths meandered between blossoming trees and flower beds; geese cackled in the distance and cattle lowed, their copper bells tolling dully as they plodded home to their snug barns; pigeons cooed and fluttered about the red-tiled roofs; tall chimneys bestowed plumes of blue smoke against the darkening skies.

It was . . . home.

They came to earth on the broad lawns before the great mansion. Rows of centuries-old beech and oak stood against a sky where flames of peach and tangerine and peacock-blue were spread like splendid Oriental tapestries. Herds of wooly sheep were being herded home; ducks squawked on small, still ponds; the reddening sun touched the old stone walls to sanguine, rich hues.

Here, you somehow sensed, reigned peace and tranquility, warmth and rest, with good country food and fine wines to be shared with friends before a roaring hearth.

"It is, dearest, everything I wished it would be," sighed Arimaspia, leaning her head on

Kesrick's shoulder. "Even Scythia may boast no finer homes than this."

"We live a bit more rudely back in Tartary, m'dear," whispered Sir Mandricardo in the ear of his Amazonian lady-love. "But you'll enjoy it nonetheless, I assure you!" he added, giving her ample cheek a secret tweak.

Callipygia giggled a most unAmazonian giggle. She was . . . very happy.

They dismounted from the Cloud, and servants came hurrying out to greet the long-delayed return of their master. Sir Kesrick had not at all been certain what to expect, but he saw happy smiles of welcome on old, familiar faces, and realized with a deep sigh of relief that Dragonrouge was still Dragonrouge.

On the front steps of the great house, however, the world of Terra Magica had yet one surprise for them. For there, resplendent in ceremonial robes of dark crimson velvet, a great gold chain-of-office about his sooty neck, stood none other than Gaglioffo.

The Paynim bowed in a low obeisance to Sir Kesrick, who stood dumbstruck, staring at him in astonishment.

"Welcome home, my Master!" exclaimed Gaglioffo. "By Mahoum and Termagant, but you will find everything exactly as it was—and the twin sacks of rubies which Your Worship left behind (rather unaccountably!) on a deserted ship amid the waters of the Middle Sea, are safely stored in your treasury, with not (I swear by Golfarin, the nephew of Mahoum!) a single ruby missing therefrom."

They gazed upon this humble, if amazing, apparition quite thunderstruck. They had, heretofore, known Gaglioffo (variously) as whimpering, cowardly, treacherous, thieving, deceitful, flattering, scoundrelly and untrustworthy. Now they perforce must consider him as chamberlain of Dragonrogue, and overseer of Kesrick's ancestral estates. The transformation was unbelievable.

Not really. It was simply that the ugly, bowlegged little Paynim had experienced a change of heart. Discovering that his Wyvern-drawn chariot had brought him to Dragonrouge, the ancient seat of Sir Kesrick's line, and recollecting that, of all the folk he had encountered across the length and breadth of Terra Magica it was only Kesrick of Dragonrouge who had treated him with any compassion, the little Paynim had taken his arrival here as a Sign.

Introducing himself as a good friend of Sir Kesrick, he had promptly taken charge of the business of running Dragonrouge. Once Kesrick had a chance to examine the books, he found to his immense relief (and considerable surprise) that Gaglioffo had been exact and scrupulous and completely honest; he had also been hardworking and rather thrifty. Never had Dragonrouge turned so remarkable a profit; never had the farms, fields and vineyards been so closely and carefully supervised; never had the rentals and taxes been so well collected, or so safely stored.

It would seem (as the author of *The True and Veritable History* remarks), that when a scoun-

Via Cloud

drel such as Gaglioffo repents, he bends all the way to virtue.*

Most of the servants at Dragonrouge were old family retainers, familiar faces remembered by Kesrick from his childhood. Without exception, they were hugely pleased at his homecoming, and the feast they laid before their master (and their future mistress) and their guests that night was a feast to be long remembered.

There was roast suckling pig (complete with an apple in its mouth), and smoking slabs of succulent beef, and trout from the mountain streams, and pheasants, and every manner of vegetable and soup and salad, and fresh bread steaming from the brick ovens, and jams and jellies and fresh ripe apricots and pears and peaches, and crusty pastries stuffed with cinnamon and spices, and thirty-seven kinds of wines, champagnes, brandies and liqueurs.

Truly, none of the adventurers had dined so splendidly since the beginning of their travels, no, not even at the wedding feast of Felixmarte of Hyrcania and the disenchanted Princess, Lunetta.

"My word!" sighed Atlantes, clasping bony hands over his small, round belly, "but you do yourself splendidly down here in the land of the Franks! I must really visit here more often."

After the desserts, and sherbets, and custards, and fruit and cheese and everything else was finished, they all trooped off to bed in one or another of the many guest rooms Dragonrouge

---

* Nevertheless, Sir Kesrick counted the contents of the twin sacks of rubies, just to be sure. *They were all there.*

contained. All, that is, but Atlantes and Dame Pirouetta, each of whom desired swiftly to return to their own residence.

After bidding their farewells to these tried and true friends, and before turning in, Kesrick and Arimaspia strolled by moonlight in the gardens, arms around each other's waist. Nightingales were warbling in the flowering trees; fountains splashed in marble basins; the night air was delicious with fragrance which the breeze wafted from the rose bushes.

"It's certainly different from Scythia, dear," Arimaspia sighed, staring dreamily about. "I shall be very happy here."

And Kesrick silently vowed to do his best that she should be.

BOOK SIX

THE ENDING OF THE ADVENTURE

26

Wedding Bells

Ten days after their return to Dragonrouge, Sir
Kesrick and Princess Arimaspia were married
by the town's chaplain, the bride unspeakably
beautiful in a close-fitting gown of ivory lace
provided by Dame Pirouetta, the groom splendidly turned out in gray velvet with scarlet
trimming. Everyone in the town or in the estate,
and just about everyone in the local countryside,
attended the ceremony, at which Sir Mandricardo served as best man and Princess Callipygia
as maid of honor.

When their nuptials were concluded, the village bells pealed a joyous salute to the happy
couple, which drove hundreds of startled pigeons into sudden flight.

Besides the Tartar knight and the Amazon
girl, other of their friends and companions at
one or another stage of their journeys were
present at the wedding. Dame Pirouetta and
the Wizard of the Pyrénées had come, of course;

so had the sorcerer Pteron, all the way from the Isle of Taprobane, which is in the seas below Hindoostan, their companion on a former adventure. Sir Felixmarte and his bride, the Princess Lunetta, were unfortunately unable to attend, being still on their honeymoon, but King Bardondon and Queen Balanice of Bohemia sent as their wedding gift a handsome flower arrangement, composed of precious gems and noble metals.

The wedding feast, if anything, truly outdid the meal the adventurers had enjoyed on the night of Kesrick's return to his estates. I will not bore my reader with a list of the superb dishes that were paraded in succession—they included, however, peacock roast, unicorn's liver in aspic, candied orchids, brisket of Sea-Serpent, nightingales' tongues, larks' brains, and several dishes hitherto unheard of, such as mangoes and ice cream, banana *royale*, and salted peanuts.

These last were from the unknown realms across the great ocean, from Manoa and the Seven Cities of Cibola, and the famous Kingdom of El Dorado. Dame Pirouetta, I suspect, had more than a hand in this; or, perhaps, Atlantes.

Throughout the sumptuous feast, Gaglioffo, resplendent in his robes of office, stood beaming, hands clasped behind his back, rocking complacently upon his heels, occasionally frowning at a clumsy servitor or pausing to sample judiciously the beverages served by the wine steward.

Suffice it to say, it was a True Feast. Indeed,

Wedding Bells

Dame Pirouetta was heard to declare that she had never eaten better, not even at the table of Haroun al-Raschid or the Emperor Nebuchadnezzar of Babylon in the days of its prime.

There were all of the usual toasts and speeches and the townschildren sang a number of old Frankish songs. The most unexpected visitors were the Red Dragon and his entire family, flown here from Mount Caucasus. Gartazascus Minor had very much wished to attend the nuptials of his friends, Sir Kesrick and Princess Arimaspia.

As even the Great Hall was too small to accommodate Gartazascus and his dragoness, to say nothing of their seven draklings, they were served the wedding supper in the courtyard, with the tall casement windows of the Great Hall opened to their fullest extent, so that the family of Dragons could share in the festivities just as if they were actually inside the Hall.

Huge troughs were hastily fetched from the stables and set before the Dragons, while Gaglioffo ordered five or six more oxen be put on the turnspit to satisfy their dragonish appetites. And, indeed, they were more than a bit hungry; it was a long flight from Mount Caucasus to Kesrick's ancestral abode.

The oxen were swiftly roasted *just right*, although in far less time than it should have taken. I suspect that Dame Pirouetta and Atlantes put their heads together to accomplish this feat. Several gallons of champagne were emptied in the drinking-troughs and the Red Dragon and his brood got more than a little tipsy, not being familiar with that beverage.

The draklings, by the way, behaved themselves admirably, and were much complimented on their table manners.

And if you are wondering what ever became of the matched pair of Wyverns, the tenderhearted Arimaspia begged her husband to turn them loose, which he promptly did. They flew off to Mount Atlas to rejoin their kind, and the iron chariot of Zazamanc became a relic, parked on the front lawn thereafter.

Atlantes, by the way, had insisted on Kesrick's retaining Brigadore. The faithful Hippogriff, he said, had by now become too firmly attached to Kesrick for them ever to be parted again.

And besides, the Wizard of the Pyrénées had plenty more back in the stables behind his Iron Castle.

That evening after the wedding feast, Kesrick and his beauteous bride bade farewell and safe journey home to their guests, all except for Mandricardo and Callipygia, who were planning to stay at Dragonrouge for the weekend, before departing for Tartary. Dame Pirouetta flew home to Broceliande on her Cloud and the Wizard of the Pyrénées returned to his Iron Castle on Hippogriff-back, while Gartazascus Minor and his family, of course, already possessed their own mode of transportation.

Following these farewells, Kesrick and Arimaspia withdrew to the seclusion of a cozy hunting lodge in the woods north of the estate to enjoy their conjugal night in privacy and seclusion.

A bit later, Mandricardo and the Amazon

Wedding Bells

strolled by moonlight in the gardens, discussing their own wedding plans. Sir Kesrick had suggested they have a double ceremony at Dragonrouge, but Mandricardo politely declined, with the warmest thanks.

"We do things a bit differently up in Tartary, you know, old boy. Gathering of the clans on the steppes, dancing around bonfires, and all that sort of thing. The Pater would never forgive me if I robbed him of the, hem, pleasures of seein' Cally and I properly tie the knot in the approved Tartarean custom, what?"

Later, as they strolled hand in hand under the moon, the Amazon girl remarked:

"It will be a long ride to Tartary from here, forsooth! Still, there's no other way to do it, and Kesrick has offered me a steed of my own for our journey . . ."

"Right-oh, pick of the stables, what? Fine chap, Kesrick," the Tartar knight added sentimentally.

"He is that and more," declared his lady-love with feeling.

"S'pose we should stop on our way and visit Amazonia, what? Tell the Queen your mother the happy news, meet all of your sisters, and so on."

"I think that would be very nice," said Callipygia.

"Who'd ever have thought that rogue, Gagli-offo, would turn another leaf and reform like that, eh?" continued Mandricardo in wondering tones. "Wonders will never cease, eh, 'pon my word!"

"It was a surprise to me, too," smiled the

Amazon girl. "Perhaps all a confirmed thief and scoundrel needs is a good job that pays well and affords him a bit of dignity. Sometimes, anyway . . ."

He gave her an admiring look.

"Got quite a head on your shoulders, m'love," he said. "Along with all your *other*, and more obvious attributes." Here he gave her a little surreptitious pinch and she squealed, and giggled, and gave the offending hand a small, reproving slap.

"Go along with you, now; someone will *see*."

"Oh, by my halidom!" he chuckled, pretending to grumble.

They strolled a bit farther, before turning back and turning in for the night.

"What *is* a halidom, anyway, did you ever manage to recall?" she asked.

"Dashed if *I* know," he confessed good-humoredly. "Hope I've got one of the blighters, though. Demned unknightly to swear by somethin' you ain't got, what, what?"

And it is at this point that the author of *The True and Veritable History of the Knight of Dragonrouge* concludes his admirable narrative, in the approved and ancient tradition, with the fine old phrase:

And they all lived happily ever after.

As with Kesrick, I present here the Notes to
Dragonrouge, and, wherever possible, I have tried
to avoid duplication of information from the
first novel. These Notes are provided so that
my reader will not have to waste his or her
time trying to figure out where I found the
source for some of my data.

CHAPTER 1.

Moghrabi Sufrah. The actual name of Alad-
    din's uncle. The African is not given in the
    text of the Arabian Nights story, but appears
    in a brief biographical sketch of this person-
    age in a delicious volume called Imaginary
    Lives by the historian Schwab, to which the
    reader is heartily recommended.
Fayoles. A king of Numidia, according to the
    historian Rabelais. Numidia itself, of course,

is one of the many nations of antiquity which did not make it into modern times.

Pappaeus. Arimaspia swears by the name of the supreme god in the pantheon of Scythia, whose worship is elsewhere forgotten.

CHAPTER 2.

Mine Host. I can't say for sure (and *The True and Veritable History of the Knight of Dragonrouge* fails to supply a name for this individual), but the description and speech patterns remind me of Long John Silver in *Treasure Island.*

Ys. A legendary seacoast city in Brittany, long ago sunk beneath the sea.

Tarshish. An ancient city in Spain, visited by both Alexander and Julius Caesar, also long vanished under the sea.

CHAPTER 3.

Mezzoramia. An imaginary country in North Africa (imaginary in Terra Cognita, at least!), described in the *Memoirs of Sig. Gaudentio di Lucca,* by S. Berington, published in London in 1737. This rare novel may perhaps be the earliest "lost race" romance ever written, and forms a bridge between the Utopian romance and the Haggard/Burroughs /Merrit lost-race yarn.

Seacoast of Bohemia. One of Shakespeare's little jokes. Bohemia, of course, was nowhere near the sea.

The Notes to Dragonrouge

Fastiticalon.   A truly gigantic sea tortoise mentioned in many of the better Bestiaries of the Middle Ages, and generally considered large enough to be mistaken for a smallish island.

Detosyrus.   Arimaspia swears here by the son of the Scythian god, Pappaeus, whose mother was Apia.

CHAPTER 4.

Skidbladnir.   A magic boat belonging to the Norse god Odin, which both steered and propelled itself, and which could expand to accommodate any number of passengers.

St. Colman.   There are one hundred and twenty saints with that name, and most of them are Irish. St. Colman Elo McBeosna Macui-Seilli of the Hy Neill tribe lived between A.D. 553 and 610 and was a nephew of the much more famous St. Columba. His feast-day actually is September 26, and, as he *did* have a run-in with the Whirlpool of Brecan, I have taken the liberty of assuming that he liked to "mess about in boats." Since hardly anything is known about him at all, for certain, permit me to presume that his nautical discoveries may have gotten confused with those of St. Brendan.

I am not making this stuff up, you know! And how he got possession of Odin's magic boat is anybody's guess. (I am indebted to my friend and correspondent, William Hamblin of Ann Arbor, Michigan, for this valuable information.)

CHAPTER 5.

Frozen Sea. For some reason or other, the Greek and Roman geographers were firmly convinced that the oceans north of, say, Iceland were frozen solid. But they're not, at least in Terra Cognita, the Lands We Know.

Eridanus. An ancient and obsolete name for the river Po.

Apia. Mother-goddess of the Scythians, wife to Pappaeus and mother of Detosyrus. I had to look all this stuff up, don't forget.

CHAPTER 6.

Atlantes. The history of this famous wizard, who dwelt in a magical castle of iron atop the tallest mountain of the Pyrenees, may be found in the *Orlando Furioso,* a work by the historian Ariosto. He was famous for his herd (or flock?) of Hippogriffs, and seems to have been a friendly sort of fellow, as wizards go. Pratt and de Camp employed him as a character in their excellent fantasy novel *The Castle of Iron.*

Broceliande. An enchanted forest in France where Sir Huon of Bordeaux met Oberon, King of the Fairies. The enchanter Merlin also lives there, under spells too powerful even for him to break. Sounds to me like just the sort of place a nice old fairy godmother would choose for her residence: such interesting neighbors!

The Notes to Dragonrouge

CHAPTER 7.

Thunderthighs. While the history of the Giant Thunderthighs seems to have hitherto gone unrecorded, you can read all about his famous relative Blunderbore in "Jack the Giant-Killer."

Felixmarte of Hyrcania. There is an old prose romance about this fellow, or perhaps one of his ancestors with the same name, one of the many written to capitalize on the success and prestige of *Amadis of Gaul.*

CHAPTER 8.

Tirante the White, et al. Tirante and Palmerin were the heroes of knightly romances written after the success of *Amadis.* Esplandian was the son of Amadis, and his adventures comprised the sequel to that famous romance, called *Exploits of Esplandian.*

CHAPTER 9.

Stumbleduffer. A rather nice, if nearsighted giant, who lives in the Zetzelstein Mountains, near Orn and Puffleburg. You will be able to read more of his history if my fantasy novel for children, *Summer Magic,* ever gets published.

CHAPTER 10.

Osmund.   A wicked magician who was the pre-
mier foe of the famous St. George; see the old
treaties, *The Seven Champions of Chris-
tendom.*

Fairy Blackstick.   Something of the history of
this famous individual can be found in *The
Rose and the Ring,* a celebrated history by
W. M. Thackeray, much admired by Andrew
Lang, who enthusiastically recommended it
to his own readers.

CHAPTER 11.

"The moon has spots . . . etc."   Actually, this
quotation does not appear in the works of
Cornelius Agrippa, but in a book called
Beyond Life by James Branch Cabell. I've a
feeling it would rather tickle Mr. Cabell's
fancy to have something of his considered as
Holy Writ.

Cornelius Agrippa.   A famous Medieval authority on ceremonial magic whose works are
still studied. In a place like Terra Magica,
where magic certainly works, I think it quite
likely that famous occultists would become
the saints of a religion based upon magic.
And Herr Agrippa is famous enough to have
become a character in Marlowe's play, *Doctor
Faustus.*

Trismegistus.   If Medieval authorities on magic
became saints, surely the old-timers would

be considered prophets. Hermes Trismegistus was the name by which the Greeks called the Egyptian god Thoth, reputedly the inventor of magic and the founder of alchemy.

"How absurd . . . etc." Not from H. Trismegistus at all, I fear, but a quotation from the *Icaromenippus* of Lucian of Samosata, the very first tale of space travel in all literature.

Althotas. A friar, or other clergy, in the religion of magic would doubtless assume a name famous from magical history; and Althotas was the magical tutor of Cagliostro.

CHAPTER 12.

Zoroaster. The founder of the Parsi religion of pre-Islamic Persia, a faith which still survives in India. The medieval writers considered him one of the fathers of magic.

"A man who can laugh . . . etc." The quotation is actually from a book by H. L. Mencken called *Minority Report.* My notebooks are full of stuff like this.

Albertus Magnus. Another authority on magic from the Middle Ages, author of many treatises on the magical or healing properties of precious stones and minerals, etc. The funny thing is, he actually *is* a saint.

"It is never too late . . . etc." The quotation comes from a book called *Year In, Year Out,* by A. A. Milne, the creator of Winnie the Pooh.

Apollonius. A celebrated magician of antiquity who was a contemporary of Jesus. Philostratus wrote his biography.

"The absence of noise . . . etc." The quotation is from Tolkien's chum, Charles Williams, but I forget which book.

Paflagonia. The scene of Thackeray's delightful treatise, *The Rose and the Ring*, a splendid spoof of fairy tales. If you haven't read it, then you must: where do you think I got the idea for *Kesrick* and *Dragonrouge* from, in the first place?

Concaline. You will find more concerning the history of this wicked fairy in Madame d'Aulnoy's story "The Good Little Mouse" in one or another of Andrew Lang's celebrated "color" fairy books.

Paracelsus. Another one of the Middle Ages' distinguished authorities on magic. His real name was Phillipus Aureolus Theophrastus Bombastus von Hohenheim; but he wrote under the name of Paracelsus—possibly, because his real name was too long to be put on the spine of a book.

"Only he who has known defeat . . . etc." The quotation actually *is* from the works of Paracelsus. No foolin'!

Merlin. You certainly must know who he is.

"Two ills . . . etc." The quotation is actually from the epic fantasy play *Peer Gynt*, by Henrick Ibsen. If you're a fantasy fan and you haven't read it before, well . . . what are you waiting for?

Mother Apia. Arimaspia here swears again by the wife of the chief of the Scythian gods.

CHAPTER 13.

Manosa, El Dorado, Norumbega, etc. All of these are imaginary countries in South and North America (which hadn't yet been discovered at the time), and which, since they never existed in Terra Cognita, never were. At least, in the Lands We know.

CHAPTER 14.

Invisible Host. I don't know what you think, but the description of the palace and of the hospitality afforded our adventurers, sounds very much to me like the palace of the Beast in "Beauty and the Beast" by Madame de Villeneuve (1740). If so, it's damn well that Arimaspia did not decide to pluck one of his roses!

CHAPTER 15.

Ctesias. As far as we know, the first writer in history to describe the unicorn. L. Sprague de Camp has a sonnet on him.
Monoceros. Probably the rhinoceros, but, then, who knows?

CHAPTER 16.

Draco ignispirans. This is the proper scientific name for your fire-breathing dragon; I am indebted to L. Sprague de Camp for the appropriate Greek, or Latin, as the case may be.

Lycosthenes, Aldrovandus, etc. These are the authors of famous books of zoology, or natural history, anyway, which was what zoology was called before it became a science. Lycosthenes was a German writer and Aldrovandus an Italian, and I really don't know about Physiologus. Anyway, they all regarded dragons very seriously, and discussed them.

Arcalaus. The wicked enchanter who is the villain of *Amadis de Gaul. Amadis,* by the way, has been rendered into decent English by Robert Southry, and can be found in your larger libraries.

Tarasque. A famous "historical" dragon who ravaged the countryside around the desert of Crau, until pacified by St. Martha, who was then converting the heathens in Arles. She doused him from stem to stern with a bucket or two of holy water, then led him tamely about, using her garters for a leash. I am not making this up.

Crysopylax Dives. His history is recorded by Professor Tolkien in a treatise called *Farmer Giles of Ham.* A dragon of ancient and imperial lineage.

CHAPTER 17.

Tamed by virgins. We know from the Bestiaries that Unicorns are; it is entirely my own notion that Monoceroses also are. But, then, who is to prove me wrong?

The Notes to Dragonrouge

I have utterly no idea why unicorns succumb to virgins. I don't, myself, but then, of course, I am a man and not a unicorn.

Emperor Contalabutte. A hot-tempered and contentious monarch who once had the audacity to go to war against Sleeping Beauty's prince (then King). He lost: Contalabutte, that is.

CHAPTER 18.

Jaunia. A small country in the Balkans once ruled by the Yellow Dwarf (see "The Yellow Dwarf" by Madame d'Aulnoy). The name of his country is not given in d'Aulnoy's text, but appears in Andrew Lang's marvelous history, *Prince Riccardo*.

King Bardondon and Queen Balanice. This royal pair appear in an historical treatise by Count de Caylus entitled "Rosanelle." You will find the story in Andrew Lang's *Green Fairy Book*. It is not said in that history what kingdom they rule, so I am pleased to flesh out the record (it was Bohemia) from *The True and Veritable History*.

Quesiton and Nacumera. All that I know about these two remote countries is that they are mentioned by Sir John de Mandeville.

Mataquin. A country mentioned in the works of the historian Perrault (see "The Sleeping Beauty in the Wood"); it was twelve thousand leagues away from Sleeping Beauty's country, which was probably in the same part of Europe as seacoast Bohemia.

CHAPTER 19.

Grumedan the Enchanter. You can read all
about him in the old French fairy tale "La
Princesse Primpenella et Le Prince Romarin,"
which, for some ungodly reason, is retitled
"Prince Narcissus and Princess Potentilla"
in Andrew Lang's Green Fairy Book. He is
large, ugly, one-eyed, clumsy, and stammers,
just as I have described him; Lang, however,
does not make him stammer in dialogue. I
have corrected this minor oversight.

Cinderella I. According to Lang, in his admirable novel Prince Prigio, an ancestress of
the royal house of Pantouflia. ("Pantoufle" is
French for "slipper," so we may presume
that the name of the country derives from the
history of this famous lady.)

Seven-league boots. I am indebted to Andrew
Lang, yet once again, for the date of Hop-o'
-my-Thumb's adventure with the Ogre. But I
strongly doubt if these are the same boots
stolen from the Ogre, as they were among
the fairy gifts given to Prince Prigio at his
christening. But then, surely, Terra Magica
contains more than one pair of seven-league
boots!

Callipygia Fecit. I am indebted to the historian Milne, in his treatise Once Upon a Time,
for instructing me in the manner in which
princesses in fairy tales sign their names
(Where would I be, without my notebooks?)

Cakes of millet flour, etc. This recipe is given
in "The Yellow Dwarf," a celebrated history

The Notes to Dragonrouge

by Madame d'Aulnoy. You will find the story in Andrew Lang's *Blue Fairy Book*.

CHAPTER 20.

Pamphyllia. An old-fashioned country in Asia Minor, long since vanished.

Pantouflia. An imaginary country; the scene of Andrew Lang's eminently readable history, *Prince Prigio*. Read it.

Crim-Tartary. You can read all about it in Thackeray's treatise, *The Rose and the Ring*. Read it, too.

Water from the Fountain of Lions. You'll be hearing more about this miraculous beverage in a future chapter, so I'll save my notes till then.

CHAPTER 21.

Senzar language. My source for this is *The Secret Docterine* by Madame Blavatsky, founder of the Theosophical Society. The book is an exhausting compendium of the sheerest balderdash.

Fairy of the Mountain. Actually, in "The Yellow Dwarf," the historian d'Aulnoy does not explain how the Princess Bellissima came by the recipe for the lion-taming pastries. Fortunately, *The True and Veritable History* supplies us with the information that it was given to Bellissima's mother by her fairy godmother, who does not seem to have been elsewhere listed in the Annals of Faerie.

Paridamie. How Dame Paridamie became Queen of the local troop of fairies is given by the historian Count de Caylus in a treatise entitled "Rosanella." You will find it in the *Green Fairy Book.*

CHAPTER 22.

Gyges. You can read about this individual in your Herodotus. His magic ring was much celebrated for conferring the gift of invisibility upon its wearer.

Doused with water. It would seem that wicked fairies are not "liquidated" as wicked witches are (according to the historian Baum) by getting wet. See the tragic end of the witch Mother Gothel, in *Kesrick.* She was caught outdoors in a sudden shower.

Surcantine. Paridamie's rival for the fairy crown in "Rosanella."

CHAPTER 23.

Pay the price for his villainies. You can read about Grumedan's punishment for this and other iniquities (and about the fairy Melinette, too) in "Prince Narcissus and Princess Potentilla" in the *Green Fairy Book.* That particular volume certainly contains a rich storehouse of fairy lore and history.

CHAPTER 24.

The Fountain of Lions. You can peruse what is known about this Fountain in a document recorded by the Brothers Grimm, entitled "The Water of Life."

Iron rod, two loaves, etc. This is according to Grimm. My research in such matters is scrupulous, even to the fact that you have to leave the courtyard of the enchanted castle before twelve o'clock, or you'll find yourself locked in.

Restored to life. Actually, the Brothers Grimm do not say that water from the Fountain of Lions revives the dead, only that it cures any illness. However, the hero of Andrew Lang's delightful history, *Prince Prigio,* employed the same Water to restore his brothers Alphonso and Enrico to life (they had been burned to ashes by a Firedrake), as well as the palace cat. I am also endebted to Mr. Lang for the correct Latin inscription on the bottle.

Put out of his misery. Grumedan was not slain or destroyed by the fairy Melinette. However, she did seal him up in a crystal globe for a thousand years, which effectively removed him from causing any more trouble in Terra Magica for quite a long time, you will have to agree.

Hyrcania. I don't seem to have mentioned yet that Hyrcania was supposed to be more or less in the same place as Germany is in our world.

CHAPTER 25.

Poictesme. An imaginary province of France in the works of James Branch Cabell. See in particular his books *Figures of Earth* and *The Silver Stallion.*

Neustria. An imaginary French province in the novels of Leslie Barringer, such as *Joris of the Rock.*

Trypheme. From Pierre Louy's romance, *The Adventures of King Pausole.*

Averoigne. Yet one more imaginary French province, this one from the short stories of Clark Ashton Smith.

Joiry. See the tales in C. L. Moore's excellent volume, *Jirel of Joiry.*

CHAPTER 26.

Manoa, Cibola, etc. Legendary countries which were formerly believed (or supposed) to exist in South America. Nobody had discovered South America yet, by the way, but Dame Pirouetta was a good friend of the Grand Inca.

Draklings. The historians Lang and Baum disagree on the proper term for young dragons. Baum prefers "dragonettes" (see *Dorothy and the Wizard in Oz*), while Lang prefers "draklings." Since this book is dedicated in part to Andrew Lang, it seems only fit and proper that we honor his preference.

Halidom. No, I don't know what the word means, either. Do you?

DAW

Presenting JOHN NORMAN in DAW editions . . .

☐	HUNTERS OF GOR	(#UE2010–$2.95)
☐	MARAUDERS OF GOR	(#UE1901–$2.95)
☐	TRIBESMEN OF GOR	(#UE1893–$3.50)
☐	SLAVE GIRL OF GOR	(#UE1904–$3.50)
☐	BEASTS OF GOR	(#UE1903–$3.50)
☐	EXPLORERS OF GOR	(#UE1905–$3.50)
☐	FIGHTING SLAVE OF GOR	(#UE1882–$3.50)
☐	ROGUE OF GOR	(#UE1892–$3.50)
☐	GUARDSMAN OF GOR	(#UE1890–$3.50)
☐	SAVAGES OF GOR	(#UE1715–$3.50)
☐	BLOOD BROTHERS OF GOR	(#UE1777–$3.50)
☐	KAJIRA OF GOR	(#UE1807–$3.50)
☐	PLAYERS OF GOR	(#UE1914–$3.50)
☐	TIME SLAVE	(#UE1761–$2.50)
☐	IMAGINATIVE SEX	(#UE1912–$2.95)
☐	GHOST DANCE	(#UE2038–$3.95)

With close to four million copies of DAW's John Norman books in print, these enthralling novels are in constant demand. They combine heroic adventure, interplanetary peril, and the in-depth depiction of Earth's counter-orbital twin with a special charm all their own.

DAW BOOKS are represented by the publishers of Signet and Mentor Books, NEW AMERICAN LIBRARY.

NEW AMERICAN LIBRARY
P.O. Box 999, Bergenfield, New Jersey 07621

Please send me the DAW BOOKS I have checked above. I am enclosing $_____ (check or money order—no currency or C.O.D.'s). Please include the list price plus $1.00 per order to cover handling costs.

Name _____

Address _____

City _____ State _____ Zip Code _____
Please allow at least 4 weeks for delivery

DAW

TANITH LEE

"Princess Royal of Heroic Fantasy and Goddess-Empress of the Hot Read."

—**Village Voice** (N.Y.C.)

☐ THE BIRTHGRAVE   (#UE1776–$3.50)
☐ VAZKOR, SON OF VAZKOR   (#UE1972–$2.95)
☐ QUEST FOR THE WHITE WITCH   (#UJ1357–$1.95)
☐ DRINKING SAPPHIRE WINE   (#UE1565–$1.75)
☐ VOLKHAVAAR   (#UE1539–$1.75)
☐ THE STORM LORD   (#UE1867–$2.95)
☐ NIGHT'S MASTER   (#UE1657–$2.25)
☐ ELECTRIC FOREST   (#UE1482–$1.75)
☐ DAY BY NIGHT   (#UE1576–$2.25)
☐ THE SILVER METAL LOVER   (#UE1721–$2.75)
☐ CYRION   (#UE1765–$2.95)
☐ DEATH'S MASTER   (#UE1741–$2.95)
☐ RED AS BLOOD   (#UE1790–$2.50)
☐ SUNG IN SHADOW   (#UE1824–$2.50)
☐ TAMASTARA   (#UE1915–$2.50)

NEW AMERICAN LIBRARY
P.O. Box 999, Bergenfield, New Jersey 07621

Please send me the DAW BOOKS I have checked above. I am enclosing
$_____ (check or money order—no currency or C.O.D.'s).
Please include the list price plus $1.00 per order to cover handling
costs.

Name _____

Address _____

City _____ State _____ Zip Code _____
Please allow at least 4 weeks for delivery